Rover's Tales

Also by Michael Z. Lewin

Rover's Tales

Michael Z. Lewin

Illustrations by Karen Wallis

A THOMAS DUNNE BOOK.
An imprint of St. Martin's Press.

Illustrations copyright © 1998 by Karen Wallis

The story "The Hand That Feeds Me" was first published in England in 1994 by Chatto & Windus in a collection entitled *3rd Culprit,* edited by Liza Cody, Michael Z. Lewin, and Peter Lovesey. "Doggy in the Window," "The Elk," "Follow the Leader," "Getting On," "The Hand That Feeds Me," "Love," "Pound," "Stand by Your Human," and "Ups and Downs" were published in England in 1994 by PawPaw Press in a collection entitled *Telling Tails.* Copyright © 1994 by Michael Z. Lewin.

Design by Ellen R. Sasahara

Library of Congress Cataloging-in-Publication Data

Lewin, Michael Z.
    Rover's tales   /   Michael Z. Lewin. — 1st ed.
        p.   cm.
    ISBN 0-312-18169-8
    1. Dogs—Fiction.   I. Title.
PS3562.E929R68   1998
813'.54—dc21   97-41881
                                                                CIP

First Edition: March 1998

10 9 8 7 6 5 4 3 2 1

With special thanks to
Liza Cody and
Peter Lovesey

Contents

vii

Contents

Rover's Tales

Pound

EVEN NOW I can't believe how stupid I was. It was the kind of mistake a puppy would make. I shiver just remembering it. You don't pick the independent life unless you know better. I wasn't even that hungry.

It was a perfectly ordinary day and I was trotting along an alley. I wasn't particularly tired. I wasn't lost in thought about higher things. It was just another summer day. And then, in my path, I found a bit of steak. Fresh steak.

On any other day in the whole of my adult life I would have smelled something fishy. But that day all I thought—and I remember it as clearly as if it happened an hour ago—all I thought was, "A stupid human has dropped something good here." So I ate it.

It's not that the steak was poisoned. I wouldn't miss something like that. The only thing wrong with the steak was that it was too good. It was a little bite of heaven.

Not far away there was another piece. I ate that too. And then another.

Bang! They had me. Out of nowhere a man in a dusty uniform dropped a noose on a stick around my neck. Another uniform jumped out, and before I knew it I was on my way to the dog pound.

To know that you've fallen for a goofy old trick like that is depressing beyond imagination. Especially for a mature dog. A dog who is sound of mind, wind, and limb. A dog at the height of his powers. A dog more accustomed to getting others out of trouble than to being in trouble himself.

THERE WERE TWO dogs already caged in the van. One, a male, was old and sick and didn't say anything. The other was a young female with a collar. She was frightened and nervous and talkative. "What's going to happen to me? Will they cut me open? Will they kill me?"

She was obviously just a "lost" dog, and she'd be home in her own basket before dinnertime. But if she'd been on the streets any time at all she would have known the answers to her questions. When dogs on the streets get together they often talk about the pound. Though it's rare to talk to a dog who has personal experience. Not many who go in ever come out again.

It's a six-day time limit in this town. They don't automatically spay or neuter you, but if no human claims you or chooses you in six days, then you make the trip that none comes back from.

I've heard that other places have different limits and rules, but that's how it is here.

WHEN THEY UNLOADED me they didn't give me the slightest chance to escape. Then they locked me in a cage. I was alone, which may sound luxurious but it wasn't. My cage was almost too small to turn around in. It was smelly, and there was nothing but a little chicken wire between me and the dogs beside me and behind me. There was chicken wire beneath my paws too, above a tray.

But the worst thing was the incessant noise. All the time, all around, there was chatter, chatter, chatter. "When's food coming?" "I want some water." "How long you been here?" "Where'd Fido go?" "Get your tail out of my face or I'll bite it off!" Day and night. Night and day.

With nerves shot by such conditions, what are any dog's chances of appealing to a human who's looking for a pet? Once in, that's the only way for a dog to get out alive.

When they locked the door behind me I curled up in the tightest ball I could. I tried to block out the racket. I tried to forget the fact that I'd let this happen. I tried to ignore how it was all going to end.

IF IT HADN'T been for the male in the cage next door, I might never have come out of my funk. Whenever he saw a human being, he shouted at it.

He didn't care whether the human was a "customer" or a hired hand. All a human had to do was put its nose around the door and my neighbor was off. "This is demeaning!" he'd call.

"We're not insects! We're not insensate beings! What about some rights here?"

He was so persistent that I began to laugh when he launched himself. Then he asked me what was so funny. "You are," I said. "You talk to them like they were capable of understanding what you're saying to them."

"Not at all," he said. "I talk to them because I am capable of understanding what I say to them."

"A philosopher. That's all I need."

"In truth," he said, "I think it is what you need. In a fix like this I'd say we all need a little philosophy."

At that moment a new human came into the room. He walked quickly up and down the rows of cages. He had a hired hand with him, and to my astonishment this "customer" chose nine dogs.

Not, however, including either my neighbor or me.

"That was a close call," the philosopher said after the humans left. "We were lucky. He was only looking for little dogs."

"What do you mean we were lucky?"

"Those poor things are all headed for laboratories," he said. "A stay of execution at best. I don't know about you, my friend, but I gave up smoking years ago."

"At least it would be a chance to get away."

"So you want to get away?" he said.

"I certainly do."

"Well then, I'd say that what you need to concentrate on is a young, insecure human child."

"It is?"

"Scarred and a little ragged around the edges like you are, you'll never get an adult to pick you. Nor are you so very big and potentially threatening that they'll see you as a watchdog. I've got a better shot at that. Neither are you small, perfectly formed, and cute, like the psychotic female in the cage on the other side of me."

"I heard that!" a high-pitched voice said.

"I hope a cat gets your next litter," the philosopher snapped at her. Then to me he whispered, "That's rather a kind wish, because it presumes she'll live long enough to have another litter. But she's too stupid to work all that out."

I said, "You were telling me I need an insecure child."

"Yes." He dragged the word out in a low rumble. "You need a child who will look at your scars and see itself."

I THOUGHT ABOUT that a lot in the night. Six days can seem forever, but when two of them go by and you've hardly even noticed, you begin to take account of time.

After morning mush the philosopher said, "You've decided to go for it. I can tell by the way you're sitting."

"There's not much good living to be had when you're dead," I said. "I hate the idea of what I've got to do, but there isn't really a choice."

"Look sharp," the philosopher said. "A little human male has just come in and any creature that ugly must be insecure."

SURE ENOUGH, THE young male and his father walked along the line of cages. I took a deep breath. Then I put my head down between my paws and watched this child as his parent led him my way. When the kid looked at me, I thumped my tail. When he got close, I whined quietly. I licked the wire that separated us.

The child stopped in front of me and put out his hand.

I had an instant, just an instant, when what I wanted to do more than anything in the world, more than life itself, was to clamp my teeth around those stubby fingers and bite. Bite for my mother, squashed by a tractor. Bite for all the broken limbs, all the tangled chains, all the caged starvation. Bite for all the dogs in this very pound. Bite for all of caninekind.

I almost did it. Almost.

But at the last moment I licked the child's fingers instead. It felt like the ultimate degradation.

The father said something to the child and then they conversed. For once in my life I knew what human beings were saying. The father was urging the child to make another choice. A better choice. He was a wiser father than he knew.

The father led the boy away.

Quietly the philosopher said, "You almost blew it, chum. I saw. But you've hooked that kid. Take it from me, Daddy could show him Lassie now, and he'll still pick you."

I was not so sure.

But the philosopher was right again. A few minutes later, the boy dragged his father back to my cage. I was nearly caught off guard but I dropped down, and whined, and thumped my tail, and did the licking thing again. The stuff of nightmares. And it became clear that the decision was made and that I would live.

The boy and his father left to complete the paperwork. The philosopher was ecstatic. "Fantastic!" he said. "Whoo-ee! I am so pleased for you!"

I admitted that I probably would feel pleased too, eventually. As soon as I had escaped from my new owners.

"One more word of advice," the philosopher said.

"What?"

"When you get away, don't let yourself get caught again. You ain't convincing enough to pull this off more than once."

"I'll remember." Then after a moment I said, "Philosopher?"

"What?"

"How long have you been in here?"

He smiled. "I have world enough, and time."

"How long?"

"I make it five days, give or take one. But mathematics was never my strongest discipline."

"Did I . . . ?"

"An ugly little kid like that would never have chosen a spectacular, beautiful, and dynamic creature like me, Rover. He is deficient in the quality necessary for such a judgment. For me, it's the best or nothing!"

Just then a hired hand came in. The hired hand was carrying a collar.

The philosopher began immediately. "Hey, what's with you beasts? Are you so idiotic, so stupid, that you cannot see beyond the noses on your snouts? To roll dice with our life and death de-means you far more than it demeans us!"

He kept it up without stopping. His voice was the last sound I heard as I was led on a leash out of the pound.

Stand by Your Human

THERE ARE SOME summer days that are perfect. They're bright and fragrant. They make you grateful that you are free. On days like that it's hard to believe that there is violence and cruelty anywhere in the world. But there is. It's the way life is.

On this particular day I found myself in a part of town that was new to me, an area where the houses each had a bit of land. I was walking down the sidewalk and I saw her.

She lay stretched out on the grass. She was in the shade of a tree, and even from a distance I could tell she was twitchy and restless, which seemed at odds with the nature of the day. So I walked over.

She didn't notice. When I was only a few feet away I said, "Hi."

She sat up. In a voice that was barely audible she said, "Go away. Don't bother me."

"That's not very friendly," I said. "And it's such a beautiful day. Look at that sky."

She didn't look up, but she didn't say anything either, so I sat down.

"Oh, don't mind me," she said. "I'm fed up, that's all."

"Troubles?" I asked.

"You could say that." She sighed.

"I don't mean to intrude," I said, "but would these be troubles caused by a human?"

"You won't lose often betting that way." She laughed. "Sorry to moan. I'm just licking my wounds."

"Literal or metaphorical wounds?"

"Both."

"The human hits you?"

She said nothing but she dropped her head to her paws.

Suddenly the day was not such a nice one. Quietly I said, "Tell me what happened."

"I was crossing the driveway, and suddenly he drove in off the road. Fast."

"He never——"

"Yes, he hit me with the car. Well, I'm overstating it a little. It was only a glancing blow and I bounced off the side, but it was as if he didn't even see me. Or, if he did, as if he didn't care."

"Are you all right?"

"Bruises. Nothing major physically. But I was so shocked! I couldn't believe what had happened."

"What did you do?"

"If I had any sense I would have left then and there. But I'm too forgiving. That's my problem. I never believe the worst of people. Well, you don't like to, do you?"

"And?"

"I picked myself up and went to him. The least I expected was that when he got out of the car he'd say he was sorry and give me a hug. I wanted to show that I didn't hold it against him. He has his problems, but he can be nice when he's in the mood, he really can. Playful, affectionate, generous. Everything you could possibly want in a human."

"But he let you down," I said. "Like they do."

"Worse than that."

"What?"

"He kicked me."

"He didn't!"

She indicated her ribs. "He behaved as if I was in the wrong. Like, I was in his way and got what I deserved."

I shook my head. "And despite all that, you're still here."

"Yes."

"Are there children in the house?"

"Two." She smiled. "You do understand, don't you."

"When you live on the streets," I said, "when you've seen some of the world, you can't help but learn about troubles. There are certainly more than enough to go around."

"Yes," she said.

"I don't look for trouble," I said. "But I hate injustice and I seem to find it everywhere I go. Take yourself. What happened to you wasn't just, was it? It was wrong, pure and simple."

"So what would you do, if you were me?"

"You could redress the balance a bit."

"I could?"

"If you were willing to accept a little help from a friend."

"Meaning you?"

"Meaning me."

"I hardly know you."

"We could correct that too."

"I don't really feel like it," she said. "Sorry."

"Okay," I said. "Back to Plan A."

"What's Plan A?"

"He dishes out the rough stuff, but can he take it?"

She opened her eyes wide. "Really? Rough stuff?"

"Sure."

"What are you going to do? Nothing too drastic, I hope. The children would be upset."

"Well, I don't plan to run him down in his own driveway," I said. "I don't have a car. But I think we can devise a modus operandi that will pay him back some of what he's owed and at the same time make things better for you."

She looked into my eyes. "You've done this kind of thing before, haven't you?"

"I don't turn my back on trouble," I said. "And I know about humans. I loathe it when they encourage us to show our loving natures, and then take advantage. More and more I've made it my mission in life to even the score. Sometimes it's a violence problem, like yours. But there are plenty of other problems, and they don't have to be big. Just yesterday I came across a pup who was looking for his ball. After some detective work I tracked down the human children who'd stolen it."

"And what did you do?"

"I . . . distracted them. When they turned their attention to chasing me, they left the ball so the pup got it back."

"I see," she said with admiration in her voice.

I scratched myself behind one ear. "You know," I said, "maybe it's just as well you're not in the mood."

"Why's that?"

"I'd probably give you fleas."

"I'm not scared of a few fleas," she said.

"I'll remember that," I said.

"My name is Pansy. What's yours?"

"I get called all sorts of things, but none of them very nice."

"Those aren't real names."

"Once upon a time, long long ago when I was little, they called me Rover."

THE TRAP WAS a simple one and we didn't have to wait long to spring its jaws. Humans being what they are, we knew Pansy's man would return to his car, and probably sooner rather than later. So we crouched behind some bushes that skirted the short path between the house and the garage.

Sure enough, the man came out and he was alone. He slammed the door behind him and headed our way.

Just as he passed me, I jumped out and bit the man on his buttock.

He screamed and whirled in shock.

I hung on for a moment, then dropped off. I improvised a second bite, deep into the man's ankle. Gratifyingly, he fell to the ground.

I ran to his head end and bared my teeth. In my loudest voice I shouted, "You are an evil disease of a creature! You're cruel and self-obsessed and ungrateful! You're friendly only when you feel like it, and you act like any little crumb of affection you hand out is a big deal!"

The man waved his arms wildly, trying to fend me off, even though I wasn't attacking. Then he began to rise.

"Now!" I called.

From her place in the bushes, Pansy ran out. She screamed at me, "You vicious beast! Get off my human! Leave him alone! If you don't get out of here right now, I'll tear you to bits!"

She was terrifying. I turned tail and ran.

IN THE ALLEY behind the human's house I sat and caught my breath. As I cooled down I became aware again of what a beautiful day it was. Dog days, some call them. And now, having righted a wrong, the day was better than ever. I felt wonderful, in the prime of my life.

A cat entered the alley from the street. It strode purposefully, like they do when they're on their way to cause some mischief. But when it saw me, it stopped. Cats are not my favorite creatures, but I don't have a thing about them. I hadn't chased a cat for the sheer pleasure of it for ages, but the day was so bright and I felt so good that I was considering it when I heard Pansy come up behind me. I only looked her way for a moment, but when I turned back to the cat it was gone. Say what you like about their personality defects, cats are not stupid when it comes to their own survival.

Pansy sat down beside me. "It worked like a charm," she said. "I shouted after you until he went back into the house."

"Did he say anything to you?"

"Yes. Nothing intelligible of course, but it was all approving, even grateful."

"Perfect," I said. "And I can't tell you how good it felt to sink the old choppers into his backside."

"And you bit him on the leg he kicked me with. I almost wet myself, it was so good to see that."

"You're in for steak tonight, my female," I said. "After all, you saved the man of the house from the savage, wild dog. In fact I'll probably be a pack of wolves when he's told it a few times."

"I really am very grateful to you," Pansy said. "If they do give me steak, let me bring some out to you."

"Thanks," I said, "but I can't stick around. Your human is probably calling the dogcatchers right now. I've got to make tracks."

"I understand," Pansy said.

I got up.

"You be careful now, hear?" she said.

"I do my best."

"And if you're ever back this way, just remember, they have me powdered for fleas twice a year."

That was certainly a thought to warm a poor rover's heart right through. I trotted away down the alley.

Goodies

I CAUGHT THE scent half a mile away. Human beings up-breeze were cooking meat outdoors. It was unmistakable and very welcome at the end of a hot day. There would be rich pickings in the night.

I followed the meat scent and came to a property that was surrounded by a wooden fence. I began to check for gaps, although I could always dig my way underneath. I didn't feel a sense of urgency. If they were still cooking, they would be eating for some time to come.

I was in the alley behind the house when I heard two human voices, both loud and angry. They were incomprehensible, of course, but suddenly two cooked chicken legs flew over the fence and landed on the ground in front of me. They were both a little burned. Maybe that's what caused the raised voices. I found them to be very tasty appetizers.

I had just finished when a small long-haired female sprinted into the alley. She must have come through a hole in the fence. She saw me and said, "Hey, you! Have you seen my chicken legs?"

"Don't do yourself down," I said. "They're short, but they're much cuter than a chicken's."

She growled. "A joker, huh?"

We both stood our ground. I saw her take in the chicken bones by my feet. But then she sat down and said, "I can't stay mad at a male with a sense of humor. There are so few of you around."

I said, "And I love a female who knows where there's a hole in the fence. I think you and I are going to get along. I'm Rover."

"My name's Dolly."

"Dolly," I said, "your chicken was scrumptious, but If I'd known you were coming I'd have saved you a bite."

"There's plenty more inside," Dolly said. "Other meat too."

"I was planning to come back in the middle of the night," I said. "Will you be around then?"

"Why wait?"

"In my experience," I said, "human beings tend to get in a lather about strange dogs."

"I know you're a stranger, and you know you're a stranger, but they don't know that," she said. "And they won't, if you go about things right."

"I like you better and better, Dolly."

"If you behave as if you belong at the party, they'll accept it. They'll think you came with someone else."

"Behave as if I belong?"

"Wag the tail. Sit up and beg. Jump up for the meat when they hold it out. All the old boring tricks."

"It sounds so demeaning," I said.

"Who is exploiting whom?" Dolly asked. "And remember, this way you're not fighting every creature and its cousin for scraps in the middle of the night."

"True."

"Just don't get aggressive and you'll have all the meat you can eat."

"I feel a relaxed mental attitude about to engulf me," I said. "So, Dolly, where exactly is this hole?"

THERE WERE A lot of people, and at first I hesitated. "I spend so much time avoiding human beings," I said. "It isn't easy for me to seek them out."

"Watch me and learn," Dolly said.

She trotted to a group of three males. She sat by one's feet and thumped her tail. The male picked something off his plate and gave it to her.

She turned around and came back to me. "See?" she said. "Easy-peasy lemon squeezy."

"Okay," I said and took a deep breath. I headed for three females and a male. I sat. I thumped tail. I threw in a mournful whine.

Sure enough, one of the females dropped half a sausage on the grass. Down the hatch. Then I thumped tail for more.

The male held a piece of burger up in

the air. "Oh dawg," I thought. But in for a prawn, in for a pork chop. I jumped and grabbed the burger. It was tempting to go for the fingers as well, but I took the long view.

Then one of the females held out a piece of meat and threw it. I chased after it and found a rather tasty piece of sheep. And, though I had to make an effort for every mouthful, soon I wasn't hungry anymore and I had eaten well. Pride is soothed by a full belly.

LATER ON I found Dolly lying under a tree. I was going to thank her for inviting me in, but I saw that she was wet and cold and angry, and she stank of something unnatural.

"They go crazy with the power," she snarled.

"What happened?"

"There I was, happily sit-up-and-begging away, when this hairy male starts waving a piece of pig in my face."

"And?"

"I'm happy to have some pig, so I beg for him. But is that enough? No. So I jump. But even that's not enough to part this male from his precious piece of pig. Next he pretends to throw it, and when I don't go for that, then he does throw it. But he throws it into the swimming pool."

"And you went in after it?"

"Don't be stupid, Rover."

"So what did happen?"

"When he saw I wasn't going to chase his silly piece of pig, this male picks me up and he throws me into the pool."

"What a catty thing to do."

"Have you smelled that pool, Rover? It's nothing like a puddle or a river. And now I stink of it."

"I can't smell it on you."

"What a liar."

"It'll go away as you dry out." I moved closer. "And you'll dry quicker if I was to warm you up a bit."

"I was in the mood," she said. "But I'm not now."

I nodded. "But I think I know what you are in the mood for."

SHE POINTED THE hairy male out to me. He was a big one and pretty frightening to look at. He also walked with an unsteady step. I took that to mean that I had to move quickly, before he fell down and couldn't get up again.

He was talking to two females. I went to them and did the begging thing. One of the females gave me a small piece of cow. Then I looked the hairy male in the eye and thumped my tail specially for him.

He liked that. He took something from his plate and held it so I could see and then he pretended to throw it.

He was grotesquely obvious, but I went along with it. I ran into the grass in the direction of the so-called throw. I conducted a search. Then I came back to the hairy male and said, "Let's play, big boy. You seem like a whole lot of fun."

He took a piece of pig from his plate and held it for me to see and smell. I jumped up and down and said, "I like to eat pig, but a big hunk of jackass would taste even better."

Every time I jumped he lifted the pig out of my reach. And then, sure enough, he led me, ungainly as he was, toward the swimming pool.

They're so predictable, humans.

When we got near the edge, the hairy male held the pig close to my nose and then threw it into the water. That was Dolly's cue to run to a position between his legs and the edge of the pool.

And instead of jumping into the water after the pig, I jumped on the hairy male. Dolly caught his feet, and he tumbled into the stinky pool. Then I jumped into the water after him. I landed on his chest, and I pushed him back down just as he was coming up.

I swam for an edge and climbed out. Then Dolly and I ran for the hole in the fence.

Human beings may love good little doggies who beg and whine and thump. But they are quick to turn on dogs who stand up for themselves. I knew that as soon as they got the hairy male out of the water, they'd come looking for me.

DOLLY AND I didn't stop till we were well away down the alley. Then we sat, more for a laugh than a breather.

She said, "Rover, you didn't have to try to drown the guy."

"I didn't try to drown him," I said.

"But you pushed him down just as he was coming to the surface."

"I jumped into the swimming pool. It was bad luck that I happened to land on him."

"What did you want to jump into the swimming pool for?"

"The water in it stinks, doesn't it?"

"Awful," she said. "I ought to know."

"Ah," I said, "but now I smell the same as you, don't I?"

She looked at me. "I guess you do."

"And wet as I am," I said, "I sure could use a little warming up."

The Frog

I WAS ACROSS from the bus station when I heard a loud yelp of pain. I looked toward the sound and saw an ocher dog sprint into the street. He didn't look to the right or the left. He didn't hesitate. He just ran.

Then two human males appeared behind him on the sidewalk. One of them held an air rifle and he fired at the fleeing dog. The dog didn't cry out, so I guessed that the human missed. I cried out though. "This way! Come this way!" And the dog heard because as soon as he got to the sidewalk he headed in my direction.

The male with the rifle raised it again, but then cars passed between him and us. I led the running dog to a gap between buildings and we dashed into it. The gap led to an alley and safety.

When we found a quiet spot, we sat down. "Thanks," the ocher dog said.

"I've seen humans do some crazy things," I said, "but I've never seen one shoot a gun in the middle of town before."

"Usually I hear him coming, but he got me up close this time," the ocher dog said. He licked himself on a haunch. "Drew blood. Want to see?"

"I'll take your word for it."

"I was asleep. I didn't hear him until it was almost too late."

"So this happens a lot?"

"More often at night, but I guess he's working days now."

"Why do you hang around there?" I must have looked puzzled. It was what I felt.

"I love the sound of the buses," the ocher dog said. "Well, love isn't the right word. I need it. If I'm away from the rumble, the vibration, and the diesel smoke for too long I get agitated. Very agitated."

All I could think of to ask was, "Why?"

"Who knows?" the ocher dog said sadly. "Who knows?" He worked at his wound again, and then he lay down. "I wonder if maybe it's something to do with the lab."

"What lab?"

"Since I was weaned I've spent most of my life in a laboratory," the ocher dog said. "There's a drug company somewhere nearby. They gave me injections and they studied what it did to my brain." He lowered his head and spread the fur with his paws. "See?"

There was a small bulb of metal in his scalp.

"I've got four those," he said, "in different parts of my head. The fur's grown back a lot and they're not so obvious now, but I was quite a sight at first."

"How did you get out of the lab?"

"Some human beings broke in at night and opened the cages. It was a big to-do—smoke and shouting and crashing glass. But I think there were more of us there than they expected, including the cats and monkeys and rats and rabbits and mice. They carried away the monkey cages, but rest of us just got chased out the door."

"I've heard about human beings doing that kind of thing," I said.

"When buffaloes fight, frogs get squashed," the ocher dog said.

"Pardon?"

"One thing about living in a lab, you meet some very interesting and exotic dogs, and you have plenty of time to talk. I miss the conversation more than anything. I was considered something of a wag in the lab, as a matter of fact."

"Oh."

He turned to lick his wound again. He said, "I left with two other dogs, but they both died."

"How long ago was it?"

"That we 'frogs' hopped to freedom? About two months."

"At least you're all right," I said.

"Am I?"

"Aren't you?"

"I just don't know," the ocher dog said. "Take last night. I was looking for something to eat behind the fast-food place at the bus station and I found a wet paper bag full of used coffee grounds. And I ate it. It wasn't that I was starving or anything, but suddenly I got this urge and I gobbled them down like they were, I don't know, raw hamburger or something. Can I be 'all right' if I do things like that?"

"You . . . you aren't pregnant or anything?"

"Wrong gender, pal," he said.

"I realized that, but some of what you hear about laboratories, and the things they get up to . . ."

"None of us ever had any stitches down there," he said. "Though I do sometimes wonder if I've got a disease or something. Well, you never know what they've done while you're unconscious, do you?"

"Not knowing's probably worse than anything they actually did." I hoped I sounded convincing.

"I do wonder sometimes about this gender thing," the ocher dog said. "Because I don't seem to . . . well, to feel like it much. You know. It."

"Oh."

"The other day this female showed up behind the bus station. And she was . . . you know, friendly. But I just wasn't interested. Not at all."

"Oh?"

"Of course I've lived a pretty sheltered life," the ocher dog said. "There's all sorts of things that normal dogs like you know about that I don't. And, to tell the truth, that does depress me. Sometimes I wonder if I'm cut out for a 'real' life, you know? I wonder if I was born for it. But I'm doing my best, and I'm still here, which is more than K23 and K17 can say. But tell me, when a female is friendly, is it normal not to be interested? I mean not at all? Or do you think they did something to me at the lab that I don't know about?"

"It's perfectly normal," I said. "You're under stress, learning to adjust to life on the outside. When it's meant to happen, it will happen."

"Oh," the ocher dog said. "That's good to know."

I said, "If you don't mind my asking, do those things in your head ever hurt?"

"Not unless I let them get too hot or too cold. Then I get cramps in my hind legs. That can be a real drag." He waited for a moment. "Get it? A 'drag'?"

I laughed for him.

He said, "So I don't go out in the sun much."

"I suppose you're not looking forward to winter either."

The ocher dog shook his head. But then he asked, "What's that, 'winter'?"

I was shocked for a moment. But as he said, he had led a sheltered life. Any dog who runs pell-mell across a busy street without looking has missed out on key parts of his education. "Winter is this thing that happens to the weather," I said. "It gets colder."

"Like it does at night?"

"Yeah. Only more so."

"Well, I'll be all right," he said. "It's always pretty warm in the bus station."

Follow the Leader

"YOU'RE TALKING OUT of your tail," Clint said.

"No I'm not!" Barko protested.

"We've all heard the stories about them," Clint said, "but I'll bet a bone that nobody here ever met one. Am I right? Am I right? What about it, guys?"

"I haven't met one," Hula said.

"I was talking to the grown-ups," Clint snapped. "You're barely out of your litter."

"I'm nearly one," Hula whined.

"And if you keep talking when you should be listening, you'll never make two."

"Sorry, Clint," Hula whispered. He crouched as the older dog addressed the rest of us.

"So what about it? Has any of you ever met a single human being you could talk to, a human being who could understand even the simplest thing you said?"

None of the pack members answered so Clint turned to me. "You've been around, Rover. Have you ever met one?"

We were in the long grass behind a factory. It was hot, even though the sun was hazy rather than bright. I'm not cut out to be a pack dog myself but when I come across a pack that isn't comprised of psychos sometimes I hang out with it for a while. It makes a pleasant change to have some company and the chance of intelligent conversation.

I said, "No, I've never met a human being I could talk to."

Clint faced to Barko, who had raised the subject. "That's Barko for you," Clint said. "Barking off because he likes the sound of his own voice."

Part of what a pack leader has to do is keep the others in their place but I wondered how Barko would take this public dressing-down. I may never have witnessed an intelligible human being, but I've witnessed plenty of fights that started for less than the way Clint talked to his pack member.

However, Barko was either unusually easygoing or he was used to being told he talked nonsense. He scratched himself. "All I said was that there might be human beings who could talk. I never claimed I knew one myself," he said. "But my mother did tell me about a Seeing Eye dog who told her that he and his blind man always knew exactly what the other was thinking."

Clint looked disdainful.

Troy, who was the smallest of the pack, said, "Barko's shooting off at the snout again, isn't he, Clint?"

Clint laughed. Troy and Nosey chimed in. So, of course, did Hula, the puppy, who followed any lead.

Barko looked puzzled but not belligerent.

"In fact," Clint said, "I think there's considerable doubt whether humans are intelligent beings at all."

The way the rest of the pack's ears stood up showed they had never heard this old saw expressed before. A cliché, the first time you hear it, is a wisdom.

It is also wise not to undermine a pack leader unless you're looking for a fight, so I sat attentively like the others.

"Human beings are good with their paws," Clint continued, obviously pleased at the response to his initial statement. "I'll give you that. In fact, they're great with their paws. Take cars, for instance. No dog could make a car. Am I right?"

There was a chorus of agreement.

"But," Clint said, "what reasonable dog would want to make a belching, growling, dangerous thing like a car? That's what I'm saying. Just being good with their paws isn't enough to prove they're intelligent, truly intelligent."

"You mean they're not?" Hula said. His voice was filled with reverence. I couldn't remember ever being that innocent. I certainly wasn't by the time I was a year old.

"They can't talk," Clint said. "And has any of you ever seen a human being do a genuinely intelligent thing? Something that couldn't be explained as natural cunning?"

Nothing came to the pack's mind.

I knew what was going to happen next, and it did. Clint turned to me. "What about you, Rover? You're a dog of the world. Do you think human beings are brainy?"

The whole pack looked my way and although there was no animosity in the question, I was worldly-wise enough not to be the kind of stranger who suggests that a pack leader might be wrong. I have enough scars already. "Put it this way," I said. "If we could do with our paws what they can do with theirs, life would be very very different from the way they've made it."

Clint nodded, though it was a moment before he said, "Exactly."

Barko, Troy, and Nosey started nodding too.

It was innocent Hula who said, "How would life be different, Mr. Rover?"

"No cars, for a start, like Clint said. Think how much safer life would be without cars."

"Gosh," Hula said. The notion was novel and attractive to him.

But however flattering the respectful and admiring tone of Hula's voice might be, it wasn't safe. I said, "That's right, isn't it, Clint?"

"What really gets me," Clint said, "is all the things that humans make and then don't use. You can't go round a corner without stumbling over some 'thing' they've thrown away or lost. It's like because they're good with their paws they have to keep proving it. How smart can it be to make all that stuff you don't need?"

I said, "I think they make things but don't have the brains to see the consequences of what they've made."

The pack looked at me again. Hula said, "Gosh," again. I wasn't certain that Clint had the brains to know that I was not making a bid to take over his pack. So I said, "It's just like you say, Clint."

They all turned back to him. Clint nodded, but slowly. And now he was staring.

Then Barko said, "What gets me about humans is how aggressive they are. They're forever shouting or fighting."

It was not a subject that I appreciated him bringing up at that particular moment.

Clint continued to stare at me. He said, "Of course we do plenty of fighting ourselves. But not often to the death."

"That's an important difference," I said. "We fight, but they kill. That makes a lot of sense, Clint."

Clint stood up. "I'm thirsty," he said.

Barko, Nosey, Troy, and Hula all stood up immediately.

I remained sitting. "Aren't you coming too, Mr. Rover?" Hula asked.

"I'm pretty tired," I said. "I'll catch you guys later."

Clint took a couple of steps toward me. "Yeah," he said. "Catch you later."

I know how the game is played. I lowered my head until I was almost lying down at his feet.

Dog above, the last thing in the world I would ever want is a pack of dozy hounds like Clint's trailing me around everywhere I went. Maybe that's why some pack leaders get crazy.

But we're not all made the same. Clint set off through the long grass content that others should follow him.

Doggy in the Window

IT WAS A hot afternoon, and by rights I should have been dozing in the shade somewhere. That's what I intended to do. I was already in a park and under a bush.

But then human beings nearby started screaming, clapping, and cheering. I tried to ignore the noise, but it wouldn't be ignored. So I got up and took a look.

What I saw was disgusting. There were two human males in the middle of a crowd, and they were fighting. It wasn't the casual knockabout that you often see men involved in. Here blood was flowing. One of the men was using a stick.

But it wasn't the blood that was disgusting, or even the unfairness of the fight. What turned my stomach was the people watching.

If I live to be fifteen, I'll never understand human beings. In my world we all have our run-ins, and I've probably had more than most. But when there's a fight you either take a side or you leave. Do humans get pleasure from watching their own kind beat each other to a pulp? If so, I don't get it.

Fortunately, what human beings do is not my business, so I left these to their fun. I set out to find a quiet place to snooze. And that's how I came to be trotting across the parking lot of a shopping center in the middle of the afternoon on a boiling hot day.

I SAW THE female from a long way off. Even though she was inside a car I could see her silky coat and shapely tail. She was lovely. Then she saw me, and she jumped and waved. I began to feel that there might just be other things to do on a hot afternoon than sleep.

I called, "I'm on my way. Yes, I am."

She shouted back to me. I couldn't hear what she was saying.

I called again, "I'm coming, darlin'."

As I got closer I made out her words. She was crying, "Help me! Help me!"

And then I understood. The car was locked up tight. The windows were closed. The sun was strong. She was baking to death.

"Help me, *please!*"

When I got to the car I stretched up and licked the glass. It was almost too hot for my tongue. I looked into the car. But what I saw was bad. The door locks didn't have little buttons she could catch with her teeth and pull. The windows had no handles she could grab onto and turn round and round. These modern cars with electric everything are death traps.

Nevertheless I tried to reassure her. I told her to stay as calm as she could. "I'll get help," I promised. And I ran to the shopping center.

THERE WAS A steady flow of humans going in and out of the center's doors. I tried to explain the problem, but it was hopeless.

I have trouble communicating even the simplest things to human beings, though you do hear of dogs who claim they understand their humans and that their humans understand them. I don't call them liars, but I've never seen such a thing myself.

The closest I came to getting some help was from a pack of females. They were loaded with bags and moving slowly. I got them to stop. Then I tried to act out what I wanted. I whimpered, ran a few steps, nodded in the direction I wanted them to come, and whimpered again. How much clearer can you get?

To be fair, there was one who seemed more responsive than the others. I won't say she understood, but she was curious about where I might lead her. However, her friends laughed and walked away, and pack instinct prevailed.

I WENT BACK to the female in the car. She was sitting quietly. That ought to have been a good sign, but in fact it was a bad one. She was just about finished.

As calmly as I could, I explained what I planned to do next. And I explained what I would need from her. She gave a faint nod. That had to be confirmation enough that she understood. I didn't have time to repeat it and rehearse her.

I left the female and returned to the little park I'd come from in the first place. I found what I was looking for almost immediately. Not the two fighting males or their sickening onlookers, but a pack of human children.

I shouted at them and got their attention. Then I threatened to eat them. If it had been necessary, I would have nipped one. But humans, especially young ones, don't take much prodding to behave aggressively. This pack was no exception. Almost as soon as I'd growled, one of them picked up a stick and threw it at me.

They chased me. Whenever I sensed them flagging, I stopped and made with the aggression again. It was easy enough to lead them to the parking lot.

When we got to the car they were in full cry. By the door, I stopped running, turned to face them, and gave them a good target. They must have thrown twenty sticks and stones. Four or five hit the car's windows.

The glass didn't break under the barrage—that would have been too easy. But I did keep these wild children screaming and throwing things until elsewhere in the parking lot some adult humans heard the ruckus and came over. Maybe it's an instinct with human beings. Maybe they have to gather if they hear a fight.

The first to the car were a male and a female. When they saw it was a pack of children picking on a poor little doggy, they shouted at the children to stop. Almost immediately the children ran away.

"Now!" I called to the trapped female. "Now!"

With a final burst of energy, she jumped at the window closest to the two humans. She cried. She clawed at the glass. It would have taken a total idiot not to know what her problem was. It would have taken a cat to ignore it.

The two humans, to their credit, were neither. They looked inside the car. They talked to each other. For a moment, I was afraid they would talk the female to death. I have seen human beings talk to each other for hours.

But then the human female gave the human male one of her shoes. The male broke a window in the car. He reached inside and did whatever was necessary to open the door. I was so relieved I almost did a somersault. The trapped female was breathing fresh air at last. She dropped onto the seat by the open door. "I'll be all right now," she whispered. "Thank you. Thank you."

Then the two humans turned their attention to me. They waved their arms and made threatening sounds. It was clear that they wanted me to go away. I was surprised, but I didn't really care. The female in the car would be all right. That's all that mattered. That and finding a shady place for a nap.

Taboo

I WAS AMBLING toward the center of town when I heard a puppy crying. I didn't stop at first. A few yowls are part of growing up, good for the lungs. But this crying persisted. It was loud and plaintive. I followed the sound.

It came from behind a large house, but I didn't see the puppy immediately. I began to wonder if it was trapped somewhere.

"Hang on," I shouted. "Help's coming."

The crying stopped, which didn't help a bit.

"Where are you?"

"Next to the garage," a weak voice said. But before I got there a small black male stepped onto the driveway. He wore a collar, and there was a rope attached to it.

I was relieved to see that he looked all right. "What's the problem, pup?"

He started to cry again. "I'm hungry."

"Is that all?"

"It's not *all,*" he said pettishly. "It's important. I'm *hungry.*"

Now that I was close to him I could see that he was very young, one of the smaller breeds, and not particularly thin.

I asked, "Don't your owners feed you enough? Is that it?"

"They're away," he said. "They've been gone three days."

I looked at the rope attached to his collar. The other end was attached to a doghouse, and in front of that there were two bowls. The bowls were empty but I could smell that dog food had been in one of them recently.

"Is there someone who brings food?"

"A neighbor," the puppy said. "And he walks me too. We go around the block, and sometimes we play." He pointed to the house the neighbor came from.

"So are you saying he doesn't leave you enough food?"

"He leaves me plenty of food," the puppy said. "But I don't get any of it!" He started crying again.

EVENTUALLY I GLEANED that twice a day the neighbor brought food and water. But as soon as the human was out of sight, a dog came in from the alley behind the garage and ate all the puppy's food.

A *dog* stealing from a puppy. I disagree with those who say it takes all kinds. There are some kinds I can definitely do without.

Tempted as I was to track the bandit, the first problem was that the little fella hadn't had a decent meal for three days. "I'll be back," I said. "You stay here."

"I'm not going anywhere," he said. He lay down and began to chew on the rope.

WHILE I ASSEMBLED a meal, it began to rain lightly. Nevertheless, there was hardly anything in the little fella's water bowl when I got back. So while he tore into the grub, I carried the bowl three houses down the street and filled it from a goldfish pond. If I'd had more time it would have been amusing to try to get a goldfish too. But there were more important things to do.

Once the pup was full I said, "Describe the dog who's been taking your food." The shower had weakened the bandit's scent, and in the alley at the back of the house I couldn't have followed the track anyway. There were a lot of dogs in the neighborhood.

"Well, he's big," the puppy said.

Just about any grown dog would look big to him. "Bigger than me?"

He nodded, but he said, "No." Then, "I'm not sure."

"But you sure it's a male?"

"Yes. And he's brown."

"That helps."

"And he's got some black and white too," the puppy said, getting into the swing.

A lot of dogs are a mixture of colors, but I wasn't getting much of a picture. Plan B. "I'll be back," I said. "You stay here."

THE FIRST DOG I found who more or less fit the description was happy enough to come to the puppy's owners' yard with me. But the way he looked around as we went through the fence made it clear that the dog was in new territory.

"Hi," he said to the puppy. "How you doing?"

"Is this him," I asked.

"No," the puppy said. "More brown."

THE NEXT DOG I found with more brown was bigger than me. I asked as nicely as I could, but he wanted to know what it was about. I decided to tell him the truth.

"Let me get this straight," the big mostly-brown dog said. "You think that I have been stealing food out of a puppy's bowl?"

"Yeah," I said. "And if you don't come with me, I'll bite your head off, tie your legs in a bow, and drag you there by the tail."

The mostly-brown dog stared at me.

I stared at him.

Then the mostly-brown dog laughed. "You're good," he said. "Where do I go?"

When we got there the puppy said, "No. More white. And smaller."

IN ALL I paraded five dogs, but none was the bandit. I called it quits.

"Aren't you going out to look for him again?" the puppy asked. He, naturally, had been enjoying it all.

"Plan C," I said. And I took a nap.

WHEN IT WAS time for the neighbor human to bring the evening meal, I hid. The neighbor dished the food out, filled the water bowl, and left. The puppy happily began to eat.

But no sooner had the neighbor's door slammed than there was a rustle in the bushes. "Get away from that dish," a deep voice said, and then from the bushes a huge mottled dog appeared. The puppy was not wrong. This dog was *big*.

But he was also old. And he walked with a bad limp.

I let him get near the dish. Then I jumped out and went for his throat.

I had him over and pinned to the ground in a moment. My jaws were in place to tear his neck out. I said, "There is no lower form of life than a dog who would steal food from a puppy."

My prisoner did not struggle. He said, "I am so ashamed."

THE OLD DOG'S problem was that he was no longer up to fighting for his food. He had come to a part of town where most dogs are owned and well fed, and there's less competition in the alleys. But it's also the part of town where human beings who throw food away are more likely to use containers it takes agility to open. What is an independent dog to do when his mobility and agility go?

He asked me himself, "What am I to do?"

"Stealing food from puppies isn't it. Do you hear me?"

"Yes," he said.

"I'll be keeping my nose out for you, old timer, and if there's even a hint that you're up to these tricks again, I'll finish you myself." I tightened my jaws around his throat and then released him. He rose very slowly.

"There are plenty of pet cats around here," I said. "You can steal from them."

"I know," the old dog said.

I suspected that he'd tried more than once and had come off second best.

The old dog must have been very hungry to steal from a puppy. But as I watched him limp back through the bushes and out of my life, I felt it would be better for him to die with a little dignity rather than come to this. I wonder if I will still feel the same if I live to his age.

While all this was going on, the puppy sat and watched.

"Aren't you at least going to eat your food?" I said.

"I'm not very hungry."

I sat for a scratch. The ironic thing was that I was starving.

"We've got one more thing to do," I said.

"What's that?"

"Watch." I started to sing, a chantey an old sea dog taught me once. I sang it as loud as I could.

Sure enough, the neighbor human's door opened and he stepped out on his back porch.

I jumped to the puppy's bowl and began to eat his food.

The neighbor human ran toward us, shouting at me. He'd gotten the general idea. I'd let him work out the details of how to protect the puppy's food from marauding creatures.

I dropped the food that I had taken into my mouth back into the dog dish. I bolted for the alley.

And then I ran, farther and faster than I needed to. It felt wonderful to be young enough and strong enough to run. It's something you've got to enjoy while you can.

Lady Legend

"IT'LL BE HARD work, Rover, but someone has to do it."

"Lady," I said, "you are such a passionate, intelligent female, I'd hate to see you wasting your time. We're not cats. We have only the one life."

"If no one tries, what chance is there?" she said with a sigh that was almost a growl. "Injustice is caused by human beings, right?"

"That's not exactly a news bark."

"Until we can communicate with them, how can we convert them to civilized behavior?"

"It just sounds so one-sided to me," I said. "What about them learning to communicate with us?"

"Are you so sure they're even able to learn to talk to us?" she said.

"They're supposed to be intelligent."

"But they can't hear the range of sounds we can," Lady said. "So that part of their brain is more limited than ours. In fact, I think that their own spoken language may not be very good. Have you watched them, Rover? You can see human beings talk for hours and still nothing gets done."

She had a point.

"In fact, I have a theory that their writing and reading thing arose in the first place because their spoken language isn't good enough. And that's why I'm trying to learn to decipher the marks they make. Eventually I want to be able to read, and write, human language."

"It would certainly be useful to communicate with them," I said. "I know I'd like to tell them a thing or two."

"I'm sure if we could only reason with them," Lady said, "they would stop doing all the stupid things they do."

"If you pull it off, Lady, you'll be up there with the legendary dogs of the past. Like my namesake, Rover the Red."

Rover was the greatest fighting dog of his era. And, frankly, more the kind of communicator I thought human beings would understand. But I didn't say that to Lady.

She said, "I am fonder of the memory of Margaret the Mongrel and Patricia the Pawless."

Margaret was torn to shreds by wild cats while defending a lair, thinking her puppies were inside. Patricia, despite her disability, led a pack of dogs that took meat from humans and gave it to the sick.

I said, "How does 'Lady the Communicator' sound?"

"I thought 'Lady Language,' " she said. "Alliterative."

She wasn't smiling, but I wasn't surprised. Dogs dedicated to great tasks rarely have a sense of humor.

"So," I said, "how is it going?"

"I've made progress," she said. "Do you want to see?"

"Love to."

We left the alley we were in and walked to some stores. Lady stopped in front of one. "Do you see that red circle on the door?" she asked.

"Sure."

"And the red line drawn through it?"

"Across the black smudge in the middle. What about it?"

"Well," Lady said, "I think the red circle and the red line mean that something shouldn't happen."

I looked at the circle, line, and smudge again. "What shouldn't happen?"

"I think this one means that dogs shouldn't enter."

"How do you make that out?"

"I think the black smudge is supposed to be a dog."

"That's a dog?"

"Come on."

She leaned against the door and opened it. We went in. The atmosphere was thick with the odors of hot, greasy foods. Lines of human beings waited to be served, showing that their powers of scent were as limited as their powers of hearing.

"What now?" I asked.

"Watch." She barked twice. Almost immediately two human males converged on us. They were making noises and gestures intended to shoo us away. We ran back to the sidewalk.

"See?" Lady said. "I've been into fourteen stores with that symbol on the door, and I was chased out of eleven of them after a few seconds. When I went into eight stores that didn't have the symbol I was chased out of only two."

"Interesting," I said.

"It's not statistically definitive, of course," she said.

"Of course."

"Now I'll show you something different." She led me to a street corner. "See those colored lights?"

"Sure."

"Well, when they show green facing us, it means the cars coming from the side have to stop. And that means it's safe to cross the street in front of them. You watch."

I watched a light turn green. I saw cars stop. I saw some human beings cross the street in front of them. "Okay," I said. "I get it."

"But it's no good just theorizing," Lady said. "We have to test our conclusions." She led me to the curb. "The next time that light turns green, we're going to run across the street."

"You mean without looking?" I thought of all the dogs I've known who were killed by cars.

"Yes. Because we know what the light means."

"Oh."

The light changed to green. We ran. But not together. Politeness demands that the female be allowed to go first.

But it worked. Cars stopped and neither of us was killed. On the opposite corner I said, "It looks like you've discovered something, Lady Language."

She smiled proudly. "I've got something else to show you, Rover."

"Okay."

She led me to a dirt parking lot. We stopped in a space between two cars. "Human beings don't always use ideograms or lights. They also have some special symbols."

"They do?"

"The symbols go together in different orders. The various arrangements have their own meanings."

"What meanings?"

"If I knew that I'd know how to read them," she snapped. "But my theory is that they use them when what they have to say is too complicated for them to draw a picture of."

"Like, 'I've been here and this territory's mine,' or, 'I'd make a great mate for a female who's in the mood'?"

"That kind of thing." Lady began to scratch on the earth. "I've learned to make some of the symbols that are used in their system. Look." She drew shapes, X, C, V, 7, H, O, S, and T. "That's eight of them, but so far I've identified nearly forty."

I thought of the enormous number of combinations you could make with forty symbols. There are a lot of meanings, I know, but I wondered if maybe Lady wasn't in danger of overestimating what human beings had to communicate. I didn't say anything, though. I had no wish to discourage her.

"Once I've learned all the symbols," Lady said, "I can begin to study how they're used. Some combinations must be used more often than others."

"Like 'I want meat,' " I said.

"And 'I want water.' That's the idea. And I already know that there can be repetitions in a given group of symbols. There must be rules for that too."

"It's quite a job you've taken on, Lady Language."

"Nobody ever became a legend without hard work," she said. "I can write more of the symbols. Do you want to see the others?" She began to draw in the dirt.

Suddenly, behind us, a car roared into the parking lot. Lady ignored it. Nobody ever became a legend without the ability to concentrate. But I saw that the loud car was headed straight for the space we were standing in.

There was no time to be delicate. I lunged at Lady. I hit her square on the shoulder and knocked her out of the way. The car missed us by inches.

When the driver threw his door open and jumped out, I ran

to his feet and screamed at him, "You violent, careless, uncaring creature! You could have killed Lady Language and all her learning. What hope for the world then?"

But instead of behaving in a guilty and apologetic way, the driver kicked out at me. He wore heavy boots. I had to jump back.

I ran around his car, intending to catch him from behind and leave a dental impression on him. His offense deserved at least that much. But by the time I got to him he'd taken a metal bat out of the car. The way he threatened me suggested he was practiced in the art of killing.

I had no option. I made a strategic retreat. He followed me. So I retreated some more.

When I returned to the parking lot he was gone. But so was Lady. At least she hadn't waited for the driver to take his anger out on her.

I tried to follow her scent, but I lost it as soon as I got to the sidewalk. I went to the alley where we'd met earlier. She wasn't there.

Lady might one day become the great teacher of human language. But I had something to teach her first—that she must never allow herself to ignore human cars and human angers, the two great killers. Not if she wanted to secure her place among the great and good.

And if Lady was unable to complete her mission to give us the tools with which civilize the human species, what hope would there be for those of us left behind?

The Hand That Feeds Me

I WAS DOWNTOWN on a hot, windless, humid summer evening. I was grazing the alleys. There was plenty of food to be had—the amount that human beings throw away never ceases to amaze me, and there's even more when the temperature is high. This particular evening the only obstacle to a full belly was the competition.

When the temperature goes up, some dogs go crazy. I've seen fights to the death over a burger roll. I can fight, and win, but I don't see the point of spilling blood over a few scraps. On hot summer nights, if I meet a contentious dog I go elsewhere.

There was still a little light in the sky when I left one alley, entered another, and found an old human male poking in a barrel. Heat can have the same effect on humans that it does on dogs so I gave him a wide berth. But the old male began to talk to me.

I didn't understand a word, of course, but I could tell that he meant to be friendly. And then he threw me a piece of meat.

Dog knows, not smart to take meat from strange men, but this old male seemed genuinely amiable. What he threw was most of a well-done sheep chop. I prefer meat rare but I sniffed the chop carefully and it seemed okay, so I ate it. It tasted good.

I stayed with the old male for a while. I'd root a bit, and he'd root a bit, and then we'd move on. Whenever he found meat on the bone he gave it to me. That puzzled me until I realized he had no teeth. So I began to push bread and burgers his way. He seemed pleased.

He even tried to make things easier for me. Behind a restaurant he took the top off a garbage can and then knocked it over so I could get in. And in an alley where two dogs were already ripping through the contents of a plastic bag, the old male shooed them away. It's not that I can't do such things for myself but it made a pleasant change to be looked after.

Finally the old male decided he'd had enough to eat. He took a blanket from a plastic bag he carried and spread it in the gap between two garages. He stretched himself out and patted the space beside him. But I wasn't ready to sleep, so I left.

I DIDN'T RETURN to the old male's alley on purpose. Things just worked out that way a couple of hours later.

He was still between the garages, but I saw immediately that something was wrong. The way he lay on the blanket was wrong. The lack of sound was wrong.

I approached him cautiously. Nothing happened. But nothing could happen. The old male was dead.

There was blood on his face. There was blood on his clothes too. Someone had given him a terrible beating.

I licked one of the wounds. The blood was dry on top, but still runny under the crust. And the old male's body was warmer than the ground it lay on. He hadn't been dead long.

I picked up three human scents, all male. The odors were fresh, hanging in the sultry air. Three males together. Three against one. One old male with no teeth who gave meat to stray dogs.

I set out to find them.

THE THREE-MALE PACK had headed away from the center of town. They stuck to the alleys, though they hadn't stopped at any of the places I, or my dead benefactor, would have.

The only time their spoor veered from alleyways was when it turned along a sidewalk toward a couple of stores. There the mixture of human scents became confusing, but I guessed that they'd gone to buy something. And, sure enough, when I checked the alley on the other side of the street, I got them again. After another two blocks I began to find discarded beer cans.

I set one can from each of the men in a place where I could find it again. Then I concentrated on following the trail. I did so with increasing confidence. I figured I knew where they had gone.

There is a long, narrow park on the banks of a stream on the southern side of town. It is popular on a summer's night and not just with humans. But my trio made finding them easy. When I arrived by the waterside, they were whooping and hollering. They were throwing stones into the air and swinging thick sticks at them. They were drunk and unsteady, and they all made a terrible din to celebrate if a stick connected with a stone.

Nearby they had made a fire. A fire! On a hot night like this.

Its flames reflected on the wet sides of beer cans that lay next to a pile of jackets.

I crept toward the young males. I wasn't quite sure what I would do. I only knew that I would do something.

It wasn't until I was close to the fire that I realized that they were burning the plastic bag that belonged to the old male who gave me meat. The old male they had beaten to death.

I felt a strong impulse to attack these young killers. I wanted to sink my teeth into each of them.

But just as I was about to make my move, one of the louts spun as he swung his stick and he saw me in the firelight. He yelled to his friends, and they reeled toward me.

For a moment I considered taking them on. But they all had heavy sticks, and I am considerably bigger than a stone. So I settled for grabbing a jacket from the pile, and I ran.

They roared as one and began to give chase. But there was no way they would catch me, even though I was lugging the flapping jacket, a heavy leather thing and not clean.

The last I heard of the three young killers was what I took for swearing as their noise floated, loud and angry, on the humid night air.

I WENT BACK to the old male. I laid the jacket by one of his hands. I pushed a sleeve as best I could into its forceless grasp.

I left the old male to make three trips, returning each time with a beer can. Each can reeked of a killer and probably also bore paw marks.

Then I sat and surveyed the scene. To me it looked as if the old male had grabbed the jacket of one of his beer-drunk attackers and not let go. Perhaps the contents of the jacket would name its owner even if the beer cans did not identify the killers.

Cowards that they were, if one of them was captured he would surely squeal on the other two.

I was pleased with my justice. I was pleased for the dead old male. I had given him teeth.

I raised my eyes to the sky, and I cried to the moon. I cried and cried until I heard human beings open their doors. Until I heard them make their way into the hot summer night to see what the fuss in the alley was about. Then I set off into the darkness.

Ups and Downs

THE RAIN EMPTIED from the sky like a river, and there was no way to keep from getting soaked. If it didn't get you from above, it came up underneath. There was water *everywhere*. There was no hiding, even if you wanted to.

I didn't want to. It had been so hot for so long that I needed to celebrate. I ran among the trees. I rolled in the grass. I soaked the water up and I shook it out again. I called out to it, "Here I am! Do your thing! Give me your best shot!" While it lasted the storm was so heavy and so refreshing that I wanted to absorb every drop. I loved it. I made love to it. I sang my love to it.

And it kept on coming. Sometimes stronger, sometimes more gentle, but on and on and on. There is nothing on earth like the feel of warm, muddy grass squelching beneath your paws. I could have run through it forever. I could have died happy.

And then I heard cries. Plaintive cries of something weak and canine.

The sound drew me to a brook. Where in the morning there had been a trickle, now there was a torrent. And on the opposite bank a small dog was clawing at the slippery earth, holding onto the branch of a bush and crying for help through his teeth.

Although I had waded across the same stream before the deluge and the flooding, now it was too wide even to jump.

The rain eased, but that was no help. It would be hours before the level of the brook receded. The little dog would be long gone by then.

I looked for some way to get to the other side. I couldn't see one, so I headed upstream. If I didn't find a tree blown across the banks then I would swim for it and the current would carry me back toward the little dog.

I found no downed tree, but there was a dead limb that stretched into the torrent from where it was entangled in overgrown shrubs. Other refuse from upstream was caught on the branch too. For the moment there was half a bridge.

It couldn't last. As more detritus became caught in the tangle, the pressure of the flowing water would increase and the temporary plug would pop. So I took my chance. I scrambled out onto the branch. I got as close to the other bank as I could and I jumped. I landed short but close enough to swim ashore.

I ran back toward the little clinging dog, fearing the worst. But he was still there, hanging on with his teeth. There was no crying, though. He didn't have the energy left for that.

I didn't mess around. I grabbed him by the loose skin at the back of his neck and dragged him onto the solid earth. He was only a pup. He curled up when I laid him down. I settled beside him, sheltering him as best I could.

56

* * *

EVENTUALLY THE RAIN stopped, and the little guy began to warm up.

The first thing he said to me was, "I think I'd have made it swimming, if I'd let go."

Only a pup, but cocky with it. I said, "You'd have been sucked under in a second."

"I'd have made it," he said again. "I think I would."

"You want me to throw you in so you can prove your point?"

I felt a shiver pass through his body. "No," he said. "But I still think I would have made it."

I smiled to myself and scratched behind one ear. "I was your size once," I said.

"That must have been a long time ago."

"One day one of my sisters and I went out exploring, and we found a stream, pretty much like this one. And it was the very first time we had seen water that wasn't in a dish or a puddle or raining on us. In fact, it was where the stream emptied into a lake. Do you know what a lake is?"

"No."

"It's like a water dish, but huge. Water as far as you can see."

"Oh," he said.

"Now my litter," I said, "was one where our mother died only a few weeks after she had us. We got hand-reared by humans, and they were nice enough, but we didn't have anybody to teach us things. What about you? Do you have a mother?"

"I do," the pup said, "but some humans took me away from her and the others, so I live alone now."

"You haven't been around this neighborhood very long, I bet."

"Not long," the pup said.

"Well, my sister and I didn't have anyone to tell us about lakes or swimming or anything, so when we found this stream, we thought we'd made the greatest discovery in the world. Water in a normal-size dish is just there to drink, but this water was made to play in. That's probably what you were doing before it rained."

The pup nodded.

"Well, my sister and I spent a whole afternoon paddling in the water. And then it started to rain."

"Like today," the pup said.

"Like today," I said. "And we didn't pay the rain any attention. We ignored it. But we shouldn't have, because after a while it rained harder than we had ever seen."

"Like today," the pup said again.

"Harder even than today. And for longer. But we still didn't make for safe ground. Do you know how to find safe ground?"

"Find it?" the pup said. "What do you mean?"

"Safe ground is up," I said. "Whenever it rains hard, go uphill. Can you remember that? When water comes down, pups go up. If they want to become full-grown dogs one day."

"Up," he repeated.

"Eventually my sister and I got scared. We went to a thick clump of grass in the middle of the stream and we huddled together and we thought we were safe. But we weren't safe. When the water rose, we were swept away. Do you understand what I am saying? We were both swept away by the river, like you almost were today."

"What happened then?"

"I was lucky," I said. "As I floated out into the lake, suddenly a big bird came down from the sky, and it picked me up and dropped me off on the firm ground."

"Wow," the pup said.

"I was so tired I could hardly breathe. If I had been in the water much longer, I would have been too tired to keep afloat, and I would have sunk, and died. That's what happens to little dogs in the water. They can be brave and strong and tough, but even the bravest get tired. And then they sink, and they die. There was never a puppy any braver or stronger or tougher than my sister. I've never seen a puppy to touch her in all my life. But the bird picked me out, and when it went back for her it couldn't find her. I was lucky. She wasn't. It didn't matter a bit how strong and brave she was. And I never saw her again."

"That's awful," the pup said.

"It was the saddest day of my life," I said, "and if there's one thing that life can provide you with, it's plenty of sad days to choose from. I don't go a single day without thinking of my sister. But at least I learned my lesson. And do you know what that lesson was?"

"What?"

"When rain comes down, pups go up."

"When rain comes down," the pup said, "pups go up."

"Today, I was your luck, your big bird. But next time, if there ever is a next time, chances are you'll end up like my poor, poor sister. And we wouldn't want that to happen, now would we?"

"No," the pup said.

I STAYED TILL he was warm again and then I sent him home. I left the brook and headed for town. The cool, fresh air had restored my appetite.

It was my lucky day too because I found half a chicken in my first alley. The chicken reminded me of the big, helpful bird, and that made me wonder what it would have been like to have had a sister.

Tooth and Claw

IT WAS EARLY evening and raining hard. I was in a part of town where a lot of the houses are boarded up, and they smell like they have been for a long time. In normal weather I'd stay outside but a deluge makes any empty house a good place to shelter and sleep.

I picked one with a hole in its wall, and I went in. The last thing I expected was that it would already be occupied. A female lay on a pile of rags and shavings. When she saw me she growled.

"Sorry," I said. "I didn't know anyone was here. I didn't mean to intrude."

But instead of answering me, she began to twist and yowl. It looked like a spasm of pain.

"Was it something I said?" I asked.

Her pain continued. "What's wrong?" I asked. "Tell me how I can help."

"You can go get yourself neutered," she said. "And take all your male buddies with you."

And then I understood. She was in puppybirth.

The pain eased. "Won't be long now," she said. "I hope."

"Good. Great," I said. It didn't seem right for me to be there, but it also felt wrong to leave her alone now that I was.

"It was that collie cross," she said. "I'm sure it was that collie cross. And where is he now, eh? You and your buddies like making puppies well enough, but you're not so interested when it comes to crunch time, are you?"

"Uh, would you like me to go look for him?"

"Oh, yeah. First left past the amusement park. I'm sure he'll still be there. I'm sure he'll care. Like you all do."

"It was a stupid thing for me to say. Sorry."

She sighed. "Oh, don't mind me. But I can think of times when being a female is more fun than it is just at the moment."

"It can't be easy doing it alone," I said. "Sorry. That was stupid too."

Another wave of pain hit her. "Oh mother, oh mother!" she cried.

I left, but I doubt she noticed.

I WENT TO the house next door, and then to the one next to that. I found an old shoe. It wasn't what I had in mind but it served. I carried it outside to a deep puddle. I dipped it and filled it with water.

Then, as carefully as I could, I took the shoe back to the mother-to-be.

"Well I'll be a tomcat's uncle," she said when she saw me. I put the shoe down where she could get at it.

Although it was awkward for her, she drank the water. "You couldn't set me up another, could you, pal?" she said.

"Of course." I brought her another shoeful.

She had a spasm as she finished the second drink but when it was over she said, "Thanks, I needed that."

"Have you been here long?"

"Too long."

"Is it . . . going all right?"

"Party, party, party," she said. "Nonstop fun." But she shook her head. "Sorry, but I'm not at my best just now. I felt it coming on a couple of hours ago, but it's taking forever. It was like this last time, and then they all came out dead." She gave a short, sad bark. "I thought that was just beginner's bad luck, but then I thought that maybe it was because the father was a boxer."

"I don't understand."

"At least the collie cross had a long snout. That's *supposed* to mean they come out more easily."

"Oh." I swallowed.

"And it doesn't feel the same as last time."

"No?"

"It feels worse. *Worse!*" She began to laugh but another spasm hit her.

When it was over, I said, "Could you use something to eat?"

"Only if I live through all this."

"I'll go out and see what I can find."

BECAUSE WE WERE in an area where no humans lived, there was nothing to eat that had been thrown away behind the houses.

But I knew where there was a food store, and I headed for the back of that. It's a popular spot for scavenging dogs, and sometimes you have to scrap for your scraps. This evening, however, the rain was so heavy that I had the place to myself and I could pick and choose.

The best thing I found was a piece of liver. It smelled fresh. I carried it back and put it down beside the female.

"Now if that isn't an incentive to get this over with, I don't know what is," she said quietly. "You wouldn't get me another drink, would you?"

I went out with the shoe and refilled it. She drank the water quickly, then had another spasm.

When it was over she said, "I thought Fang. Fang, and Claw, and Howl, and Rip. That's for the males. For the females I thought Snap, and Bite, and Bark, and Growl."

"Short, sharp, and friendly, huh?"

"Except the first female out gets named Get-off-Me-or-I'll-Kill-You. How does that sound? Direct enough? To the point?"

But before I could answer she was in pain again.

When it stopped she asked, "So what's your name, big fella? Good Samaritan? Altruist?"

"They call me Wouldn't-Get-on-if-You-Begged," I said.

She would have chuckled, I'm sure, if she hadn't gone into spasm again.

When it was over she said, "I can feel them on the move. It's time for you to get out of here. This is female stuff."

"Okay. Good luck." I turned to go.

"But I'm going to call the first male Dark Stranger after you, dark stranger. If we all make it."

"I'd like that," I said. "Thank you."

Wags

I WAS NEAR the center of town in the middle of the day when I saw a three-legged female limping along a sidewalk. I wasn't sure where she was trying to go—the sidewalk edged a graveled area with nothing but a statue in it—but she seemed to be having a terrible time. I went over and asked if she wanted some help.

In a low, clear voice she said, "Go away."

Some dogs are too proud to accept help, even when they need it. I may have been guilty of that once or twice myself. I said, "What?"

"Get out of here!" the female said. "Now!"

I didn't understand but she had made her wishes clear. So I left, but I watched her from a distance.

The three-legged female continued to limp along the sidewalk, barely able to move. Whenever a human being approached she whined piteously. Many of the humans slowed or stopped. Some tried to make friends by patting her. And by giving her food.

In a comparatively short time the three-legged female begged herself a luxury meal. No scrounging in garbage cans. No fighting for scraps. I'd never seen anything like it.

I was about to head on my way when one of the female's human benefactors left her and walked into the street. There the human hailed a police car. The human pointed back to the sidewalk where the three-legged female was wagging her tail for someone else who had squatted to pat her head.

Then I saw the pitiful, hungry, deformed female notice the police car. A moment later she was three-legging it in the opposite direction.

I ran after her, but I only caught up when she stopped for a breather in an alley four streets away.

She said, "Sorry I was so rude back there, but you would have queered my pitch."

"No problem," I said. "You were hustling a meal. And doing a wonderful job of it, if I may say so."

"Thanks. But you should have seen the dog who taught me how. He was a real artist."

"How do you mean?"

"Okay," she said, sitting down. "This is how it works. Human beings have a generous side, but they need to feel that it won't be exploited as a weakness. So, for a start, I only use places where they can see me as they're walking in my direction. That way they can see that other humans ahead of them are slowing down."

"And that makes it easier for them to slow down too," I said.

"What they see is a poor, deformed little doggy. At first they can't tell if the doggy is sick. If it is sick, they don't want to know. But then they see that the doggy wags her tail for every little bit of food. They see that the doggy doesn't ever bark or bite or ask for more. They see that the doggy doesn't follow after anyone who's fed her. In fact, they see that the doggy is the perfect recipient for any generous impulse they might have."

"However small it may be," I said.

"Oh, they do like being generous," the female said, "as long as they're certain the situation won't get out of paw."

"How long have you been doing this?" I asked because I hadn't seen her before.

"Just since spring. I used to have an owner before that. And I liked him. I went everywhere with him, even to his job. That's where I lost the leg. Some jerk on the assembly line played a joke that went wrong." She shrugged. "But then last winter my owner lost his job, and not long after that he died." She laughed, but sadly. "One of those tales you've heard a hundred times, I'm sure. Look, I've made myself sad. Do you feel like a walk?"

"Sure."

"My name's Triple."

"Rover. Pleased to meet you."

WE SPENT THE rest of the day together. We watched some men bounce a ball and throw it into a hole on a wall. We watched three human children taunt a fourth until it cried and ran away. We met a pedigreed male in a wire pen who bragged about all the females he'd had. We watched two human males stagger and try to fight each other and not do it very well. And we talked about the independent life.

Once, just to see if I could, I tried to beg food following

Triple's instructions. It didn't work. I didn't get a single morsel. It was humiliating.

"Am I too big?" I asked. "Do I look too healthy?"

"It's not that," Triple said.

"What then?"

"It's in your eyes, Rover. You don't mean your wags. And your whines sound more like growls."

Later we wandered along some alleys, nosing through some trash bins and plastic bags. I get most of my food from humans too, but at least I don't have to pretend to like them to do it.

And it was in an alley, behind a big house, that we found four dead kittens in a paper bag.

They were tiny, newly born, and wet. "Drowned," I said.

"And each one with four legs," Triple said. "What a waste!"

"Maybe they were the wrong color."

"Or gender."

"Or maybe they didn't know how to make it easy for their humans to be generous enough to let them live." I gave myself a shake, but it didn't make me feel any better. "They never even got to open their eyes."

"I do believe you're a romantic, Rover."

"You don't think the humans in this house would have acted any differently if they were puppies, do you?"

She stood silent.

"I'm going to bury them," I said. "I don't want the rats to get them."

She helped me dig a hole. We dropped the four little kitten bodies in. We covered them well.

We were both getting hungry, but bags behind big houses had lost their charm and Triple didn't feel like being nice to humans. So we left the alleys and eventually found an easy meal behind a pizza restaurant.

When we finished, Triple said, "The way I beg may not have much dignity, but you don't get many ugly surprises."

"I heard of a dog who was poisoned by something a human gave him in the street."

"Oh, like I need to hear that!"

"Sorry," I said. "Sorry. I'm not in a very good mood."

"You're crying over spilled kittens, but there are a lot of worse things than that in the world."

"I know."

"Like what happened to the guy who taught me how to beg," Triple said. "You'd have liked him, I think. His ears were all chewed up. He'd lost a lot of the hair on his head. His tail looked like it was half falling off. But he was really as strong and healthy as any dog I've ever known." She sat, and I watched as she twisted around to scratch herself. Not so easy when you have only one hind leg.

She said, "His name was Carl. When he went into the pitiful act it was a masterpiece. When I watched even I wanted to feed him."

"What happened to him?"

"Hit by a car. Carl was crossing a street. There was plenty of room. But the driver veered and hit Carl on purpose."

"No!"

"It's hard for me sometimes to remember that humans aren't all like that car driver," Triple said. "It's one of the reasons I beg. Their generous impulses need to be encouraged."

"I am sorry," I said.

"Carl took a day to die," Triple said. "A whole day. It like to broke my heart." She sighed. "Broken heart. Three legs. It's surprising I'm here at all."

"What upset me wasn't the kittens," I said.

"Could have fooled me."

"Life is life, and death is death, but there ought to be more respect for the miracle of it all than bodies in a paper bag."

"And drivers who hit dogs on purpose."

"Triple, what would you say to doing something pointless, dirty, and nasty?"

"I'm not in the mood to make puppies, Rover. But thanks for asking."

"No, no. I mean something vengeful and spiteful and against human beings."

"Ah, now for help with that you've come to the perfect three-legged dog."

WE RETURNED TO the alley where we'd found the kittens. We dragged all the plastic bags of garbage we could lay our teeth on to the front porch of the big house the kittens had been behind.

When the pile was huge, we broke the bags open. Then we took some rotten meat and laid a scent trail back to the alley. Triple and I don't eat rotten meat ourselves, but we agreed it was the kind of scent that cats like. And if not cats, then rats.

It was very late when we finished, and we were both exhausted. But as we stood in front of the big house admiring our repulsive revenge, it was all we could do to keep from laughing.

"Come on," I said. "There's nothing that discourages cats and rats as much as giggling dogs."

We ran away down the street, howling with laughter. We found an open space with some bushes and settled down for the rest of the night.

We slept like puppies.

Word of Mouth

I WAS DRINKING from a fountain in the middle of town when a dog I know named Pal ran up and said, "Hey, Rover, come on! They're giving away fresh cow over behind the market."

"What?"

"Yeah, fresh cow, cut up in little cubes."

"Who is giving away cow?"

"Some human beings. There's plenty for everybody. I figure they're dog lovers of some kind."

"And I'm a green fire engine," I said. I turned back to the fountain, took another drink, and considered going in for a dip.

Pal was still there. "Honest, Rover. Everybody's talking about it."

"The heat's getting to you, Pal. There's no such thing as a free cow."

"I was only trying to put you on to a good thing," Pal said.

"Free meat is the oldest dogcatcher trick in the book." I ought to know.

"I'm not stupid," Pal said. "But I heard it from Ruby. You know Ruby? She went there yesterday with two males who'd been there the two days before. She told me herself, the cow tasted great, nobody got sick, and nobody tried to catch them."

"If human beings are giving away cow, then there's got to be some trick, some angle."

"Suit yourself," Pal said. "But I'm going."

"Good luck," I said.

"All the more for the rest of us," Pal said. He trotted off toward the market.

I drank some more water and then dipped my head in it to cool off. I met Pal last year and I've run into him only a few times since. But if he was still around he must have something going for him. Independent dogs don't last long if they don't have an edge.

If free cow wasn't being used to trap dogs, it had to be some other kind of scam. But it wasn't one I knew, so I decided that I ought to take a look.

I APPROACHED CAUTIOUSLY and stood well away. But everything appeared to be happening exactly as Pal described. Behind the market there were four young human beings in white jackets. Two were dishing out cow, and the other two, carrying clipboards, were making notes.

I counted nine dogs, including Pal and Ruby. They were all gobbling the cow as if they'd never eaten cow before. While I watched, two more showed up. And I noticed that the two humans with clipboards were counting the dogs the same as I was.

And all four humans were talking to each other. They seemed animated. Something dodgy was up for sure.

In the next few minutes another three dogs appeared. The recorders took a lot of notes. The cow chuckers chucked a lot of cow.

Then one of the recorders looked at its watch and said something to the others. In a matter of moments they had packed up and retreated inside the market, taking their stocks of cow with them.

The dogs chatted among themselves for a while, perhaps hoping the young humans would come out again. The latecomers complained that they'd hardly had any cow at all. Others told them they should show up earlier tomorrow. It became clear that these human beings dispensed cow at the same time each day. It wasn't for long, but while they were there it was all-you-can-eat. And the more dogs there were, the more cow they dispensed.

After a few minutes the group broke up and began to go its several ways. I went over to Pal. "I see you decided I wasn't so crazy after all," he said when he saw me.

"Just checking it out."

Pal said, "Have you ever had fresh cow, Rover? I mean cow that is *really* fresh." He licked his chops. "I've eaten about everything in my time—even some human, though he was already dead. But there is nothing, *nothing* to beat the taste of fresh cow."

"Well, enjoy it," I said.

"Still not convinced?"

"It means there's more for the rest of you," I said. And since it was a thought he had uttered to me only a little while before, he agreed enthusiastically.

I couldn't tell Pal what was wrong, but something was. So I stayed away.

Two days later Pal could tell me what was wrong him-self.

I SPENT MOST of the intervening time in a park where I met an extremely congenial female who had broken free from her owner and was celebrating. She was only a young thing but it was love at first scent. She told me that she preferred an older dog because an older dog could teach her new tricks.

However, afterward, as we dozed together in the park, she got "found" and I got chased away. I don't know if I taught her anything that she didn't already know, but she laughed at my jokes, and I laughed at hers, and I was sorry that something so nice ended that way. But life is short and we'd had a real good time.

I made my way back into town. And who was the first dog I ran into? Pal.

Pal was not happy.

I could see why. He had a pink plastic collar around his neck.

"What's *that* about?" I said.

Pal threw his head from side to side. The collar looked loose enough, but he could not have been comfortable with the indignity of the thing. "Don't say it," he said. "Don't say a word."

"Tell me," I said.

"It was yesterday. The cow cubes were drugged. We ate. We went to sleep. We woke up with collars."

"At least you woke up. At least you're still free."

"Yes." He was silent for a moment. "Oh, I feel so stupid." He had a furious but pointless scratch at the pink collar. "What's it all about, Rover? And how in Dog's name can I get this abomination off my neck? It's driving me absolutely crazy. It not only itches, it hums. And half the time when I stop somewhere one of those fiends in white jackets turns up." Pal looked around. No fiend was in sight. "First they feed us. Now they drive us mad. Why, Rover? Why?"

I considered. "It could be that your young white-jacketed cow chuckers are doing a research project."

"A what?"

"The humming in your collar might be a signal to them that says where you are. You and the others might be teaching them where independent dogs go to eat and to sleep."

"But why? What's it to them?"

"Don't count on it being so they can provide you with fresh cow more efficiently," I said.

Pal clawed at his new collar. "Isn't there some way to get it off, Rover?"

"But pink is such a good color for you."

"Not funny."

I examined the collar. "Bad news. It's not the kind with a buckle. It looks permanently attached."

Pal looked at me. "Is that supposed to be a joke too?"

"Unfortunately, no."

"Oh Rover," Pal whined. "Do something. *Please!*"

THERE IS AN area near the center of town where all the houses have been remodeled. The houses aren't new but the paint is lick-fresh. I led Pal to them.

"What's here, Rover?"

"Just do what I tell you," I said.

"Anything."

"First, shut up."

Pal shut up.

I found what I was looking for, a low wooden fence with boards held together by nails. With some prying and pushing, Pal and I got the bottom end of a vertical slat free from the horizontal bar holding it in place.

"Now," I said, "we slip that slat through your collar."

Pal looked at me in horror. If he did what I told him to he would become attached to the fence and at the same time he would nearly choke himself to death.

"Do it," I said. "But be careful of the nail, and be careful not to free the top end of the slat."

Pal did it, though it caused him some pain.

"Now," I said, "as soon I'm out of sight, you scream and cry like you are dying."

"That'll be easy enough," he said.

And I explained my plan.

PAL'S HOWLS BROUGHT a human female running from the house. At first the human tried to free Pal by taking the slat out of the collar, but with every tiny movement Pal screamed like he was about to die. As per instruction.

Then the human studied the collar. I had hoped she might find a way to undo it that I couldn't see, but she didn't. Instead she patted Pal's head a couple of times and went back into her house. But she wasn't there long. She came out again with a pair of scissors and in an instant Pal was free.

Having acted like a sniveling, pain-crazed pet of a dog, Pal ran for it as soon as the collar was off.

We met up in a nearby alley.

"I can't thank you enough, Rover."

"The best thanks you can give me is to tell your collared colleagues to get free the same way you did. The humans will assume a gang of nasty children is attaching dogs to fences—they know only too well what their young are capable of. But it won't do any of us any good to let the white jackets know where we go and what we do."

"Right," Pal said. "I'll spread the word."

"Meanwhile," I said, "I'm feeling hungry. How about you? There's a steak restaurant near here. Want to come with me? I had half a steak au poivre there once, and the sauce wasn't too creamy. And if we're lucky maybe we'll find a little steak tartare."

"Not funny, Rover," Pal said.

"Gee, I thought it was," I said, and I ambled on my way.

Easy Meat

THEY WERE VERY young for independent dogs. One was all brown and the other had large brown spots. I first saw them when they were being chased away from a garbage pile by a human with a broom. The second time was later the same day, exploring an alley, and I noticed then how thin they both were.

So I went over to say hello. But when they saw me coming, they backed away and were about to run when I called out, "Hey, I'm not going to hurt you. I just want to talk."

"How do we know?" the brown one said.

"Yeah, how do we know?" the spotted one echoed.

I shrugged. "Because I say so."

There must have been something reassuring in the way I spoke because they both sat down. I walked up and sat too.

"You guys been together long?" I asked.

"Forever," the spotted one said. "We're brothers."

"Yeah, forever brothers," the brown one said. He turned to the spotted one. "Give me four."

"Four," the spotted one said. They raised paws and touched them together.

"Do you say everything twice?" I asked. "I know I have two ears, but I only have one brain, so you only need to say things once."

"We do say things once," the brown one said.

"Yeah, we do."

"One time each," the brown one said. They touched paws again.

I gave myself a good scratch. "How long have you been on the streets?"

"About a month," the spotted one said.

"About——" the brown one began, but I turned to him. He stopped.

"Good," I said. "If you're hungry, come with me."

"We're hungry," the brown one said. "We're really hungry."

I TOOK THEM to the back of a delicatessen that throws away sliced meat when it's past its sandwich-by date. The meat's bagged in plastic, not boxed in metal.

There were three scrawny strays there already but I cleared them away. "Haven't you heard?" I growled. "Today is Litter-hood Day. Now clear off!"

The brothers feasted. They ate as if they hadn't had a decent meal in days. They ate as if they didn't expect another one soon.

"This is great!" the brown one said. "I was starving!"

I looked at the spotted one. "You were starving too, right?"

He just nodded. His mouth was full of sliced turkey breast.

When at last they were full we went to a stream for a drink of water. "I think I'm going to burst," the spotted one said.

I looked at the brown one. "Yeah, me too," he said. Together they said, "Thank you, Mr. Rover," and we all laughed.

Then we stretched out, and they told me how they came to be independent.

IT TURNED OUT that their owner moved houses only a few months after their mother had their litter. That's always a bad idea. Females who move house that soon after litterbirth are significantly more likely to become stressed and snap-happy than those who stay put. I know because I talked once to a dog who had done an extensive survey. Some of the guys thought he just did it to ingratiate himself with the females, but he certainly seemed to know his cranium from his kibble.

Whatever the generalities, moving house when they were so young was a particularly bad idea for these brothers because their owner crashed his car on the way. He was killed. So was their mother and all of her litter, except them. Their box broke open and they were smart enough to run. Moments after they got out, the car burst into flames. That left the two pups on their own.

I thought they'd done well to last as long as a month. Life on the streets doesn't favor the weak, even when they come as a set. Their survival showed they had something about them, that they could work as a team and that they weren't stupid.

On the other hand, they weren't eating regularly. I said, "What are you guys going to do for food till you get big enough to hold your own in a fight?"

"We've been thinking about that," the spotted one said.

"But we haven't decided yet," the brown one said.

"You could look for a berth with some human beings," I said.

"We thought about it, didn't we?" the brown one said.

"But we've heard that humans send dogs away to a place called the pound."

"And kill them!"

"The dog pound can also provide dogs with owners," I said. "And you guys are young enough and attractive enough that you'd almost certainly get permanent homes that way."

"But after all we've been through," the spotted one said, "we want to stay together."

Which seemed more than fair enough to me. And the chances of their going together from the dog pound to a single home were slight.

"We did hear about something else we could do," the brown one said. "Just yesterday. Didn't we?"

"Yeah," the spotted one said. "We heard about a place where there's lots of fresh meat, every day."

"Just waiting to be picked up."

"We were talking to this old guy. Maybe even older than you. And he told us that if we go away from the middle of town there are trees and birds and all stuff like that, but we'll find streets too. That's what the old guy said, didn't he?"

"He did," the brown one said.

"And," the spotted one said, "out there the wild animals cross the streets and get killed by cars."

"Fresh meat!" the brown one said.

"All we'd have to do is pick the meat up off the roads."

"And we'll never be hungry again," the brown one said.

"Yeah, never hungry again," the spotted one said. "Oh, excuse me."

"What?"

"We don't mean to have bad manners. You can come too, Mr. Rover. In fact, that would be really nice. I'm sure there's enough meat for all of us."

I said nothing.

"Is something wrong?" the brown one asked. "Isn't there meat on the streets like the old guy told us?"

I stood up. "There are a lot of places where you often find freshly killed animals on the roads."

"Yes!" the spotted one said. They touched paws.

"But . . ." I began, and they stopped celebrating immediately because of the tone of my voice. No, they weren't stupid.

"But," I said, "a lot of the dead animals on the streets out there are dead dogs."

"Oh!"

"Oh!"

"We couldn't possibly eat them," the brown one said.

"You are missing the point," I said. "Being killed could happen to you."

"We'd be careful," the spotted one said.

They were very young but the cavalier attitude made me angry. "Do you think only dogs who are careless get hit?"

"But cars make noise," the brown one said.

"You can hear them coming," the spotted one said.

"Think it through. There you are. You've just found dead . . . owl, or mouse, or deer. You're happy. You're deciding whether to drag it somewhere safe or to have some now, because you're so hungry. That's all the distraction it takes for you not to hear the next car coming."

They sat solemnly.

"Or suppose you hear the next car and he doesn't."

They looked at each other.

"Think how you would feel if you were looking at him dead on the road."

"Not very good," the spotted one said.

"Yeah, not very good."

"It only takes once," I said. "And boom."

"Maybe it's not such a good idea after all," the brown one said.

The spotted one nodded. "But we do get awful hungry here in town, Mr. Rover."

The brown one nodded.

"Time for Plan B," I said.

WE SEARCHED UNTIL we found an old man feeding pigeons clustered around his bench.

"There you go," I said.

"We tried to catch pigeons once," the brown one said, "but they were too quick for us."

"Not the pigeons," I said. "The old man."

"Oh I don't think I'd want to eat one of those," the spotted one said.

"Not to eat. What you do is make friends with him. Wag your tails. Pay him attention. There's nothing an old human likes better than attention. If he talks to you, great. But even if he doesn't, follow him home. Most old human beings live together in packs. If this old human doesn't want you, you're almost certain to find one or two others who will be glad to keep and feed the pair of you. And if it doesn't work out, you can always run away and try another old human."

The pups looked at each other. "Sounds good to me," the spotted one said.

They touched paws.

THEY APPROACHED THE old man on the bench. I waited long enough to see them receive their first pats on the head. Then I went on my way. Adopting an old human might or might not be a solution for them, but I've known too many dogs who died on the streets to like the idea of these pups trying their luck in the suburbs.

But I had one consolation. Even if they succumbed to the lure of easy meat they would never be left with one of them looking down at the car-struck body of the other. No, they'd never be far enough apart to be hit separately.

The Barbarian

I DIDN'T DO much that was wrong. Although I was hungry, I was careful of traffic when I crossed the street. But as I turned toward the alley I started thinking with my belly instead of my brain. There'd been good smells in that alley earlier in the day but then I was more concerned with a friendly female than with food. Now it was time. Come to papa, you tasty morsels.

So I trotted straight around the corner—and straight into trouble. Six dogs stood surrounding a cat. The cat was hissing. The dogs were taunting. And suddenly I was in the middle of the whole thing. Sometimes I wonder how I've lived this long.

"Well, well, well," said a huge, muscular dog. He was all brown except for a big white spot on his back. "I think the kitty's found itself a buddy."

"Hey," I said. "I'm nothing to do with this."

"You weren't," the enormous brown dog said, "but you are now."

The other five chuckled and already I knew that they were a pack, that the brown dog was their leader, and that they fully intended to pull me to pieces just for the sport.

Too many packs these days operate at the lowest level instead of the highest. A group of dogs *ought* to be able to pool its resources and use the strengths of each for the benefit of the whole. Packs used to work that way, but nowadays more and more pack leaders are fearful and suspicious and aggressive, and their followers reflect them. Maybe it's because there are so many humans around now and they are so hostile to independent dogs. But whatever the reason, this kind of pack brings out the worst in its members. That makes it a danger to dog and beast.

When the cat saw that the pack's attention had shifted to me it made a dash for the gap between the two smallest dogs in the circle.

Bad move.

Small dogs are quicker than big ones, and they often feel the need to prove their worth. But I doubt the cat felt anything. After its body was tossed in the air a few times, the small dogs left it. The cat was no longer the main event.

The big brown dog said, "We have bigger game today." To underline his point he lunged and snapped at my shoulder.

I was alert enough to avoid a serious bite, but he still drew blood. And there's nothing a vicious pack with a crazy leader likes better than blood. The dogs in the ring all took a step closer.

A fight is a just a fight. I've been in plenty, and I'm no pug. Muzzle-to-muzzle I was confident I could hold my own against the big brown dog. But there was no way I could take on the whole pack. I needed an out.

So in my most aggressive voice I said to the brown dog, "What's your problem, Spot?"

There was a collective gasp.

"He called him Spot."

"He called him Spot!"

One of the little dogs said to the leader, "Did you hear what he called you, *Prince?*"

But Spot had heard me well enough. And if there's one thing that dogs with spots don't like . . .

I took a step forward. "Speak up, Spot. I didn't hear your answer."

"Prepare to die," Spot said. He was blazing angry. So angry he was looking only at me, speaking only to me. That's not how pack leaders normally comport themselves.

"Up to a fight, Spotty?" I asked. "Well that's all right by me. But I'll tell you now, I'm no cat."

"Give us room," Spot rumbled. "This one's mine."

So at least now I had a chance.

The two pack members on either side of him made space. Spot crouched, like we do when we're about to do battle.

But instead of doing the same, I sat down. And I began to sing. "Moon up above, moon of my love, leap high as a bunny, make sure to come running, to me when you can, get away from your man."

Spot didn't know what was happening.

I sang louder. "Moon up above, moon of my love——"

Spot stood up. "What the *hell* do you think you're doing?" he asked.

"You said I should prepare to die," I said. "Where I come from this is how dogs begin a fight they might die in."

"Well stop it!" Spot said.

"But it's how we do things where I come from."

"Where's that?"

"Oh, far away from here." In my loudest voice I sang, "Moon up above, moon of my love, leap high as a bunny——"

"You already did that bit," Spot shouted.

"It's got to be done all the way through from the start."

"I've never heard of anything like that," Spot said.

"Would you believe," I said, "that I had never seen a cat before I came to this town? Can you imagine it? I grew up where there were no cats. Funny old world, eh?"

Spot was not amused. He crouched aggressively again.

"Moon up above, moon of my love, leap high as a bunny, make sure you come running——"

I was interrupted again, but this time it was from another direction. Two human males ran into the alley through a gate. They were shouting. And they were both carrying sticks.

I didn't get a word of what they said, but if there is one thing all dogs understand it's that when human beings with sticks appear, dogs disappear.

And Spot may have been crazy but he wasn't stupid. He realized in an instant that I'd tricked him. That I'd been singing in order attract the attention of the human beings whose houses we were behind. That I'd been trying to annoy them so they would break the fight up and save my skin.

And if there is anything a crazy pack leader with a spot on his back hates more than being called a silly name, it's being tricked in public.

"You're cat food if I ever see you again," he said to me. But he turned and he ran.

The pack ran with him.

I ran too, the other way.

But Spot only half understood what had happened. Sure, I

wanted the fight to be stopped before it started, but I also hoped that these humans would call for the dogcatchers.

A pack with a crazy leader is dangerous. Today it was sport with a cat, and with me. But what would happen if this pack cut a human child out from its herd and toyed with it?

I don't much like human children—most of them seem to be vile, brutish little creatures. But if a crazy pack did to a human child what this one did to the cat, there would be trouble for all dogs like me. Dogs running free. Dogs beholden to no one. Dogs who come from far away and sing our own songs.

The Ear

THE SMALLER DOG screamed at the house, "Stupid and ignorant creatures, that's what you are."

"Both of you are utterly devoid of cultural capacity," the larger dog called.

The smaller dog shouted, "You ought to be pegged down in a tray of cat litter with nothing but recordings of tomcat yowls to listen to."

"That was a good one, Dickory," the larger dog said.

"Thanks, Winesap," Dickory said. "It just came to me."

"Ah, the mystery of creativity," the larger dog said. At that moment a shoe passed by his nose. "What the feline!"

"How dare they throw one of their smelly paw covers at you!" Dickory said. He turned to the house and howled, "You're both vile and insensitive and undeserving and—"

He took a second shoe smack on his nose. "Oh!" He whimpered pathetically and crumpled.

I was on my way to nowhere in particular when I witnessed these events. As the small dog lay on the ground I trotted over. The larger dog was saying, "Come on, Dickory. Get up. Please, get up."

"Is he all right?" I asked.

But it was the small dog on the ground who answered. "Of course I'm not all right," he said. "My spirit ails."

Behind him a door of the house they'd been shouting at opened. A round, hairy-faced human male came out. He carried a broom and waddled down the path toward us. I said, "Guys, might I be so bold as to suggest a tactical retreat?"

"Wise counsel," the larger Winesap said. But it was the small, ailing Dickory who was first into the street as we fled.

WE STOPPED IN a vacant lot three blocks away. I said to Dickory, "I'm glad to see the shoe didn't injure you."

"It had a crepe sole," he said. "No problem."

Winesap said, "Isn't that tree beautiful?"

"What?" I said.

"The way it stretches, open-armed to the sky." Winesap sighed.

Dickory said, "It has a magnificent shape."

I looked at the tree they were talking about. I hate not to appreciate quality, but it just looked like a tree.

The small dog introduced himself. "I'm Dickory."

"And I am Winesap," the larger dog said. "And you would be . . . ?"

"Rover."

They both lifted their eyes. "Oh my, oh my," Winesap said. He swished his tail.

Dickory said, "Nothing personal, Rover, but your name doesn't put one in mind of the finer things in life, does it?"

"And were things so fine back at the house you just left?" I asked.

"Touché, Rover," Winesap said. "Point taken."

"We were there only for a day," Dickory said, "but that was twenty-four hours too long."

"I did have an inkle when we first passed their back porch that something might be amiss," Winesap said.

"But they were friendly at the beginning," Dickory said. "Weren't they?"

"Exceedingly friendly," Winesap said. "At the beginning."

"So what went wrong?" I asked.

The two dogs looked at each other. "The real problem," Dickory said, "was that they do not have the ear."

Before I could ask which particular ear he meant, the two of them put their heads together and began to sing. "When the tree, falls in the woods, there's none but me, 'neath the hoods, of the evergreen shrub, rub tummy rub."

And then they stopped. "Well?" Winesap said.

"Well what?" I said.

"Did you hear?"

"The voices, Rover, the voices!" Dickory said. "Have you ever heard a pair of dogs harmonize like that?"

It was true, I hadn't. "Never," I said.

They began again, "Hey little female, what's that waggin'. Don't give up now, we can't have laggin'."

Dickory said, "If you know it, feel free to hum along."

"But not too loud," Winesap said.

I didn't know what to say. I decided on, "I'm not very musical, but thanks."

"Not everyone's blessed," Winesap said. "Possibly you have other talents."

"Possibly."

"Which is more than those cloth-eared human beings we just left do," Dickory said.

I said, "What exactly happened there?"

"They invited us to sleep the night in their garage," Dickory said.

"On dirty blankets," Winesap said.

Dickory said, "Then this morning the male invited us onto the porch for breakfast. And as we ate——"

"While we were *eating*," Winesap said.

"The female opened the piano and started clawing it. Oh, it hurts to remember the sound even now. So raucous. So grating."

"And then she sang, Rover," Winesap said. "She sang."

"If you choose to call it that," Dickory said. "So we did the only thing we could."

"We would have been happy to be left in peace to eat, but life must be civilized."

"So we left our food and began to sing along," Dickory said.

"In retrospect it may have been unduly optimistic to think she could learn," Winesap said, "but one can but try."

"It was out of charity, Rover," Dickory said. "Strictly a freebie, but the male acted like he enjoyed the female's yowling."

"It must have been pretense," Winesap said. "How could anyone enjoy *that?*"

"Whatever," Dickory said, "but we'd sung only a few bars when the male tried to get us to stop. Inconceivable as that may be."

"But if we have a fault, Rover," Winesap said, "it is that we spare no effort when it comes to culture."

"So you didn't stop singing?"

"To tell the truth," Dickory said, "we stepped it up a bit, didn't we?"

"We did," Winesap said.

"Threw in a little counterpoint too."

"But the humans didn't like it?" I said.

"Before our very eyes," Winesap said, "the same gentle creatures who gave us milk and meat became vicious, noisy, and irrational. Everything you hear about human beings but hope you'll never experience yourself."

"They were odious!" Dickory said. "They chased us out. We didn't even get a chance to finish eating."

"We are martyrs to our art, Rover," Winesap said.

"Because we *are* great singers," Dickory said.

"Immodest it may sound to say so," Winesap said, "but fact is fact."

"How many dogs do you know who can syncopate?" Dickory said. "Who can sing overtones?"

"It is arguably the highest of the canine arts," Winesap said.

"If only we could find the right situation," Dickory continued, "then we could become the best duo ever. Better than Sonny and Ike, better than Curly and the Woof."

"What is the right situation?" I asked.

"Somewhere we can sing, day and night," Dickory said. "Artists must work to develop."

"But artists must also eat," Winesap said, "without scrounging in alleys, or being exposed to the elements."

"Fellas," I said, "I may just know a place that would suit you."

I TOOK THEM to a building in grounds bounded by a wire fence. It's not a prison—or a pound. The gate is always open, but there is a boundary. On the way I explained what I had in mind. When we got there we went in through the gate, and we waited.

Eventually we saw three young humans walking together. They were talking and didn't seem to be going anyplace in particular. "There you go, guys," I said.

"Are you sure about this, Rover?" Dickory asked. "They have sticks."

"Just let them see you, and then do all the submissive things that human beings like so much. The low posture . . ."

"The raised eyes," Winesap said.

"The thumping tail," Dickory said.

"Then," I said, "sing to them."

Dickory looked at Winesap. "I guess it's worth a try," he said.

"For our art," Winesap said, and together they trotted out to the three young humans.

I watched as they did the submissive things. I watched as they began to sing. "Gather round humans, hear as our song, tells of the open road, it's so so so looooong!"

Which turned out to be no understatement. But after the sixth verse one of the young humans approached Dickory and patted him on the head and touched his throat.

Another of humans knelt by Winesap and touched his throat. I heard Winesap falter. "Keep singing," I shouted.

They did, and the young humans took turns feeling each dog's neck. And at last the song came to an end. The critical moment.

But the young humans behaved as I'd hoped. They patted Dickory and Winesap and encouraged them to follow as they began to walk toward the building.

Winesap shouted to me, "It's working, Rover."

"You've done a service for all of caninekind!" Dickory called. And then they caught up with their new benefactors.

"Just keep singing to them!" I shouted.

Winesap and Dickory turned at the sound of my voice. But the young men did not.

I may not be a star of canine song, but I have sung to the human beings in this particular place myself. Sung enough to realize that it is a school for young humans who are deaf.

But Dickory and Winesap were in hound heaven. No matter that they had exchanged one place where the human beings did not have the ear for another.

Rage

I WAS IN an alley, looking for a little late supper before I turned in. It was night, and dark. Most of my menu examination had to be done by nose.

Although the alley was a weave of the scents of other dogs, I had no competition. They would all be bedded down in their cozy humanmade dens. By the time the nights become dark it's primarily rodents and cats who are there in the flesh.

So I was caught by surprise when I pressed my nose against the warm side of a dog. I had smelled him, of course, but assumed he was elsewhere. And I hadn't heard him. That was because he was making hardly any sound. He was barely breathing.

"Hey, are you all right?" I asked.

"No," he said. The voice was faint. I could just about make him out between piled bags of garbage. "I'm dying."

"What happened?"

"Kicked. Beaten. A stick. The lot." He paused every few words to find breath.

I said, "I'll clear these bags away and get you out of there."

"No," the dying dog said. "No." And then he said, "I don't hurt anymore." And after another moment, "It won't be long now."

"But who did this to you?" I asked, even though the answer was obvious. There are a lot of ways that a dog's body can be broken: falls, vehicles, even fights. But only one creature throws a dying dog into a pile of garbage.

"My man. Beat me." With a little surge of energy he said, "Pepper, next door, warned me. She ran away. Her man beat her. Beat his female too. And the children. Pepper said my man watched hers kick her. My man laughed. She told me to come when she left. I should have. I should have."

Then the dying dog coughed. He said, "Out of it soon. Out of it."

And then he died.

It was a terrible moment. I didn't even know his name. But there was no learning it now.

And it all made me so *angry*.

I looked up and saw the back of the house that must belong to the dead dog's man. It was divided, two houses in one building. The other, presumably, belonged to the neighbor who beat not only Pepper but his own female and his own litter.

I'll never understand human beings.

But the hot, liquid anger that flowed through me congealed into a sort of plan. It wasn't perfect, but I had to do something.

I walked through the open gate toward the house of the dead dog's man. It had a small porch. So did the neighbor's house. Only a low fence divided the two backyards.

At the steps leading up to the dead dog's man's porch I sat

down. I cleared my throat. I shouted, "Hey, human male inside! You are a foul and rotting excuse for a life-form! Do you hear me? You must be brain-dead, if you had any brain in the first place. A cat understands the dignity of life better than you do!"

Then I stopped. I jumped the fence between the two yards and sat at the foot of the neighbor's stairs. I screamed, "You're as bad as he is, you litter of a devil and a demon." And I went through the same sort of thing that I had begun next door, louder if anything.

Then I crossed the fence and found a place where I could give equal attention to both sides. And I started again. I howled, "The two of you are candidates for excreta of the year awards, except neither of you has the capacity to understand what it's given for."

The first light to go on was in the neighbor's house. Soon a light went on in the dead dog's man's house too.

The neighbor came out onto his back porch. With the light behind him I couldn't see his face, but his silhouetted gestures were not friendly. He shouted at me, incomprehensible words. He threw an empty bottle at me. It wasn't even close. I howled louder.

Then the dead dog's man came out of his back door. He carried a thick stick that looked like an ax handle. He waved it at me. I paid more attention to him than to the neighbor. This man had already proved that he was capable of killing a dog. But I kept howling.

When the neighbor saw the man with the stick he shouted at him. That distracted the stick man's attention from me. He shouted at the neighbor. The neighbor shouted back.

I edged forward. And when the two human males seemed fully occupied with each other, I attacked the dead dog's man. He never saw me coming. I bit him on his lower leg. I bit deep. He fell down. He banged his head, a bonus. He dropped his stick.

Then I turned to the neighbor. I bared my teeth and growled and jumped the fence, but he got away from me and my vengeance by retreating into his house.

The dead dog's man was still on his porch. He held his head with one hand and his leg with the other. But I did not return to him. I moved down the yard toward the gate to the alley. My idea was to make the despicable beings angry and then leave them nothing to vent their rages on but each other.

The neighbor was gone so long I feared he wouldn't come back. But no lights went out in his house and eventually he came on to his porch again. And I could see that he now had a stick of his own, and his stick was rifle shaped.

I ran the few final yards to the alley. The neighbor fired at me three times, but only one shot was close.

When I was more than a block away I heard what sounded like another shot. That may just have been wishful hearing, but it certainly pleased me at the time.

Shot

I WAS CROSSING a street, right in the middle of town, when I heard a gun go off. I looked toward the sound and was horrified to see a dog stagger, stumble, and crumple to the ground. I ran immediately to where the dog lay, aware that although there were many human beings nearby not one showed the slightest concern. Well, what do you expect. It was only a dog.

"Can you hear me?" I said as I got there. "Can I help?"

The victim was a female. She moved her muzzle, just a bit. She whispered, "Go away."

"What?"

"Go away. Can't you see? I'm playing dead."

And then a human male got to us. He shouted at me, quite ugly sounds. He kicked at me. So I went away, but I didn't go far.

The sidewalk on which the female lay circles a tall shaft that seems to stretch into the sky, perhaps a monument of some kind, although as far as I'm concerned only human stupidity would rate a monument *that* high. But there are steps that lead up to it, and by going to the top of them I had a good vantage point. And what I saw was the "wounded" female get up and walk with the male who had shouted at me to a group of several human beings. It was clear that nothing was wrong with her. In fact, she moved most attractively.

After a while, she shook herself, paused, and then trotted back to where I had found her. There was another shot and the female "died" again.

The humans chattered for a moment. Then they began to move several bits of equipment. The male who had shouted walked to the "dead" female, clipped a leash on her collar, and led her to a box. He attached his end of her leash to something and went away. It seemed like a good moment for me to go down and have a word. Maybe she'd appreciate knowing that I've managed to untie a leash or two in my time.

"Oh, hi," she said.

"What's all the rinky-do?" I asked.

"It's acting," she said. "I'm in a commercial." She licked the fur smooth on one of her paws.

"In a what?"

"Some human beings want to sell something to other human beings. To do that they make a little movie. I'm not quite sure what they want to sell with this one, but I think it's a medicine."

"For dogs?"

She laughed. "No. Silly boy."

"They film dogs to sell medicine for human beings?"

"Sure. It's called showbiz."

"But . . . what is it that you do?"

"I've been trained to do almost anything."

"How do they train you to sell medicine?"

"Silly boy," she said again as she began to work on another paw. "I've had lots of different roles. Today it's being shot in a commercial, but tomorrow I might be in an advertisement photograph, and the next day I could be in a TV miniseries or a major motion picture. I've played them all, I assure you. And some of the costumes I've had, my *dear!*"

"Costumes?"

"Sometimes human beings want me to wear clothes like theirs. When that happens they have a clothesmaker specially for me."

"But if you're wearing clothes," I said, "how do you scratch?"

"You don't scratch, even if you itch," she said. "It's called acting."

"And that's what the training is for?"

"Among other things. But I can stand up, sit down, turn right, turn left, run, stop running, turn around, pick up what's in front of me, beg, lie down, cover my eyes, roll over, look sad, wag my tail, jump up—"

"Die?"

"They love it when I die," she said. "I get asked for that a lot."

"And you do all that to order?"

"Sure. They use whistles and gestures to let me know what they want me to do."

"I think I get the picture," I said.

"*Picture?* Hey, that's pretty good," she said. "So, what's your name, big boy?"

"Rover."

"I," she said, "am Mitzi Ritzi."

"Oh."

"My original owner called me Jane, but I don't answer to

that now that I'm in the movies." She looked at me in an appraising manner. "You know, you're nice looking, Rover."

"Thanks. You're not bad yourself."

"Oh, I wasn't thinking of that. I've been spayed."

"That's a disappointment."

"I wasn't very happy about it myself, at first," she said. "But after a while I began to look on the bright side. You get treated very well in this business, believe me. I get great food. I get washed and massaged every day. I have a vet with warm hands. So I'm not that badly off. And I have the body of a dog a year younger than I really am."

"Well, you do look great on it," I said.

"I was thinking, you might be good in pictures yourself," she said. "They could probably use a strong, rugged type."

"I'm flattered."

"But I'll give you a tip. Don't learn the tricks too quickly."

"No?"

"While they're training you they give you treats to eat. So drag it out, even when you understand right from the start what they want. Most of the time the poor dears are so painfully obvious about it all you'd have to be stupid not to get it. But if you learn too fast, you just spend more time stuck in your pen."

"Pen?"

"Oh, it's big and comfortable. I even have a TV."

I wondered if there could possibly be a pen big enough for me to be comfortable.

"And don't worry about me having been spayed," she said. "I don't think they do it to the males."

"But you're not sure?"

"You know," she said, "I do work with males sometimes, but to tell you the truth, I haven't really noticed."

At that point the humans making the commercial changed

the kind of sounds they were making. Mitzi Ritzi said, "I think they've finished the next setup, so I'm about to be on again. This is the dream sequence. I sniff something in a bag and then I dance on my back feet. Are you going to stay around? When my human tries to drive you away again I can whine like it upsets me. If I lay it on thick enough, I'm sure I can make him understand. Then we can get you a test to see if you have a future in the business."

"I appreciate the suggestion," I said, "but I don't think I'm cut out for showbiz, or the easy life."

"Well, it's no fur off my tummy, but I've enjoyed talking to you."

"Me too."

"So, tell me. How do I . . . ?"

She posed for me.

"You look wonderful," I said. "Absolutely wonderful."

Thunder

IT WAS EARLY evening on a stormy night. I was on my way to visit a friend who'd just had pups. I wanted to see if there was anything I could do for her. I also wanted to see what the pups looked like.

But as I turned a corner I all but ran over a dog lying in the gutter. His hind legs stuck out to the side, one resting limp on the other. It was clear that he had been hit by a car, that his back was broken. I recognized the smell of death about him before we exchanged a word. He was young, less than a full year.

"Hey," I said.

After a moment he said, "Hey."

"Is there anything I can do for you?"

"I don't know." Then he said, "Where am I?"

I looked around. "This road runs toward the river from the park with the rectangular pond."

"Ah. I'm in a road."

"So, how are you feeling?" I said, though I was unsure that I wanted to hear the answer. If he was in agonizing pain, if he asked me to drag him out to where another car would cut his suffering short, I wasn't certain that I could bring myself to do it for him.

But he said, "I'm a little tired."

"Then why don't you have a nap?"

"Good idea. I'll have a nap."

"Tell you what," I said. "There's an alley just around the corner. I'll see if I can find something there that will keep you warm."

"I know that alley," he said. "I was in it this afternoon."

"Yeah?"

"I found a trash can that smelled really meaty but it had a lid on it."

"That's a shame," I said.

"I do feel cold," he said, "now you mention it."

"I'll be back soon."

"Has it stopped raining?"

"For the moment, yes."

"Oh, good. I don't like rain much."

I DIDN'T WANT to spend long in the alley. What I had in mind was an old blanket, but I couldn't find one.

It crossed my mind that it would be a nice gesture to skin a couple of cats. A toasty warm muffler of cat fur would be a stylish way to send the youngster out. But there's never a cat around when you want one.

What I found was two old shirts. They were made of some unnatural fiber. Wool or cotton shirts would have smelled more comforting to me, but at least these were dry. And there wasn't much time to be fussy.

As I returned to the gutter I was afraid he was already gone. I whispered, "Hello?"

But he opened his eyes and said, "Hi."

"I didn't know whether you were asleep or not."

"Resting," he said. "And it helped. I don't feel so tired now."

"Good." I arranged the shirts on him. "There you go."

There was a blinding flash of lightning and shortly after it a vibrating crash of thunder.

"Just as well you're awake," I said.

"Why? Oh, the thunder," he said.

"Isn't it always the way? Loud noises at the very time you want to go to sleep."

"Do you know any stories?" he asked.

"What?"

"My mother used to tell us stories at night."

"Oh, right, sure. Just give me a second to think of one," and in that second I panicked because, despite all the dogs I've talked to, all the stories I've heard, I couldn't for the life of me remember a single one. I said, "Did you hear about the dyslexic agnostic with insomnia?"

"No."

"Used to stay up all night worrying if there was a God."

He said nothing for a moment. Then he said, "Oh." Then, "I had something a little longer in mind."

"Okay," I said. "No problem. But first, you remember that trash can from this afternoon? The one that had meat in it?"

"Oh, yeah."

"You couldn't get in because of the lid, right?"

"Right. The meat smelled great."

"I've got a little tip for you."

"What?"

"When there's a lid on a trash can it's natural to try to claw it off. But if you push up instead of down—with your nose or a paw—most lids will come loose."

"I'll try to remember that."

"Good."

He closed his eyes. "Do you have a story to tell me?"

"One time," I said, "I met this amazing female. She was in a pen, and she had the longest, silkiest fur I'd ever seen."

"Wow."

"And I said to her, 'That's amazing fur,' and she said, 'It's because I'm pedigreed.' "

"A snouty one, huh?"

"The snoutiest I ever met," I said. "And as well as having really long fur, inside her pen there was a house."

"A house?" he said quietly.

"It looked exactly like a human's house," I said, "but smaller. So I asked her, I said, 'I suppose being pedigreed you're so valuable that your owner lives in the pen with you. But that house looks kind of little. So is your human a miniature variety?' But she just lifted her snout in the air and said, 'That's not my human's house. That's *my* house.' 'Ooooooh,' I said, and then I started laughing. I laughed and laughed, and it made her mad! Can you believe it? She had met so few dogs in the street that she really thought that I thought her owner lived in her doghouse!"

I stopped. He didn't say anything. His eyes were closed, but I could see the shallow rise and fall of his breathing. I sat and watched him. I felt light rain on my back.

There was another flash of lightning, even brighter than before. Almost immediately there was a rattling clap of thunder.

But it didn't startle him. As the echo of the thunder stopped, I saw his chest lift and shake, a larger movement than before. And then his breathing stopped.

I stayed where I was, watching him. The rain became harder. There was nothing I could do, but still I sat. Water began to run in the gutter. Then a puddle began to build up around him.

There was nothing I could do.

The rain became a torrent.

The puddle became a lake.

Suddenly I jumped up. I ran into the road, straight up the middle. I screamed, "Where's the lightning? Bring on a car! Here I am! I'm alive! Come on, prove that I'm not!"

Hailstones joined the rain.

But I kept on running and kept on screaming, "Is that the best you can do? Is that your worst? Come on! Give it to me! I'm still here! I'm still alive!"

Doogoo

I MET HER by chance. It was night and raining hard, and I was looking for a dry place to lay my weary head. I slipped into an abandoned garage behind an abandoned house. And there she was, curled in a corner.

I don't like to intrude on another dog's space, but the rain was heavy and had already gone on more than a day. "Hi," I said. "How you doing?"

She flinched and drew herself into a ball.

"Hey, I'm not going to hurt you."

She whispered something. I couldn't hear what and shook my head. "The rain," she said.

"Yeah," I said, "it's still coming down."

"The pound pound pounding. I hate it. It sounds like cars."

"It does?"

"Their engines. The roar roar roaring. I hate cars. I can't stand them. I . . ." Her voice trailed away.

It is hard to get away from cars in a town. And at the moment it was hard to get away from the rain too.

She began to shake.

"Are you cold?" I asked. "Or hungry?"

"No," she whimpered. "Scared."

"You're safe from cars in here."

"I know," she said faintly.

"And the rain will stop eventually. I promise."

"Yes."

"I could stay with you till then. Would that help?"

"Yes," she whispered. "Thank you."

"It might be good if we talk," I said. "Keep your mind off the noise. I'm Rover."

"Sheba," she said.

"So, Sheba, tell me about yourself."

SHEBA'S TROUBLES BEGAN when she was given to a child for its birthday. Unfortunately, what the child wanted was an electronic game called Assassins. And the child was not the kind to settle for its second choice.

Time and again the child and its parents squabbled about who would feed Sheba and take her for walks. More than once the child tied Sheba to a tree and went off with its friends. Then the child locked her in a closet in order to play all day with a neighbor's Assassins and forgot about her.

When the child's father discovered what had happened, human nature took its course. The child got an Assassins of its own and the child's mother drove Sheba miles away and dumped her.

"I still have nightmares about that drive," Sheba said. "We went a long way, and then suddenly she stopped the car and opened the door and pushed me out. Before I understood what was happening, she was gone."

"Leaving you to fend for yourself," I said, nodding. I can't remember how many times I've heard variations on the story.

"All I had left was the roaring in my ears as she drove off. It was the first time that I'd really heard the sound a car engine makes. It was awful. And then, everywhere I turned there were cars and buses and trucks and motorcycles." Sheba buried her face in her paws.

I moved closer and nuzzled her. "But you're still here," I said. "You've come through."

She took a deep breath. "I couldn't bear to be near cars. So I did my prowling at night, when there are fewer of them around."

"That sounds sensible."

"Then, a few days ago, I fell asleep in what I thought was a field. But I woke up to the sound of loud, horrible engines. Cars were driving round and round and round me, and they screeched and roared, and every time I tried to run away another car came so fast I knew if I crossed in front of it I would die."

"Oh, Sheba."

"At last they stopped for a while, and I ran and ran and ran until I was exhausted and dropped on the ground. But now I shake when I hear a car, even its slightest growl. I can't help myself. I want to curl up and hide."

"How long have you been in here?"

"Since yesterday, when it started raining so hard. The pounding, and the thunder . . . It all sounds like *them*. My head snapped." She sighed. "Oh Rover, I do hate myself for being so pathetic. I'm sure if I could just get my head straight I'd be fine.

Maybe, somewhere, there's a place where there aren't any roaring car engines."

And where it doesn't rain? I thought. But I said, "I'll think about it. Meanwhile, why don't you cover your ears and get some sleep. I'll make sure no cars get you. You'll be safe."

IN THE MORNING it was still raining but I crept out of the garage. I hunted up some food and brought back a decent meal, but it took me longer than I expected. Sheba was already awake.

She did not look a well female. "You were gone," she said.

"For food," I said. "If you're going to feel better, you've got to eat."

"Food doesn't take the cars away."

"I've been thinking about that," I said.

"You know a place where there are no cars?"

"I have an idea that might help. You eat. I'll go out and see if I can set it up."

I'VE SOLVED A few dogs' problems in my time, but how do you eliminate a fear? It was not really my territory. But there are dogs around who take an interest in such things. The most famous is Young-Joy, a female whose wisdom is legend. I'd never met Young-Joy but I did know another dog whose special qualities might just help. He's called Doogoo and when I left Sheba I headed for town and asked every dog I met if it had seen Doogoo.

I always got the same answer. "What do you want Doogoo for?"

Everybody knows Doogoo. Nobody looks for him. But Doogoo does take pride in his understanding of dog psychology. He's the only dog I know who talks about edible complexes and tail envy. He is forever trying to interpret hidden motivations. And he asks endless probing questions.

I couldn't be sure that Doogoo would help Sheba, but it was worth a try.

I finally found Doogoo in a park. He was watching an ants' nest although the rain was still falling hard. I did not approach him quietly. He is a big dog and sometimes snappy from all his thinking. As I sat down I said, "Fascinating creatures, ants."

"Aren't they!" he said as he turned around. "Such social organization. Rover! Long time no scent!"

The way to deal with Doogoo is to be direct and to be first. If he begins to talk about what's on his mind, only the deaf survive without severe pains in the brain. I said, "Doogoo, listen to me. There is someone I want you to help. I am going to lead you to her. On the way you will say nothing to me. *Nothing.* Get it? If you so much as warn me that a lion is about to jump on my back, I will rip your tail from its stump."

He looked bemused at first, but then he said, "Rip my tail off, eh? Yes, it is a rather fine and enviable tail, isn't it?"

I kept him moving fast. Dogs who talk a lot rarely run a lot. Before long he was short of breath.

SHEBA WAS EXACTLY where I'd left her. And she was shaking, though it wasn't cold.

I went to her and said, "I've brought someone who might help. Talk to him. Answer his questions. Don't be afraid. He's an oddball, but he won't hurt you."

"All right," she whispered.

I called Doogoo in and he approached her slowly. Gently he said, "You're going to be all right. I'm certain of it. I know about these things."

I had to give it to him, he had a good lairside manner.

He said, "Before we consider the noises that upset you so much, I'll need to know more about you. May I ask you a few questions?"

Sheba nodded.

"Other than this phobia of car engines, do you consider yourself to be a normal dog?"

"Yes," Sheba said.

"You were owned until a few weeks ago, right?"

"Yes."

"During that time did anybody ever call you obediencely challenged?"

"Uh, no."

"Was your bark like other dogs' barks?"

"I guess so."

"Did you ever think of yourself as alternatively bited?"

Sheba's eyes widened.

"How do you feel about your tail?"

Sheba looked to me.

I left Doogoo to it.

THE RAIN HAD all but stopped. Often after a heavy rain I go to a river or a stream. They swell and sometimes overflow their banks and leave good things to eat. It is my ambition one day to catch a live fish for myself, but the best fish I've had so far have been washed up after heavy rain.

This day, however, I stayed near the abandoned garage. I didn't do much other than enjoy listening to creatures that are usually silent go "squish, squish" as they ran around on the wet earth.

But I must have dozed too, because I was taken completely by surprise when Sheba whispered in my ear. "Wake up, you louse."

"What? Oh. Hi. Nice to see you out and about," I said.

"After a couple of hours listening to your friend Doogoo I *had* to get out of there."

"Didn't he follow you?"

"I outran him."

"Dashed across some streets, did you?" I asked. "Hid behind some cars?"

"You knew exactly what you were doing, didn't you?"

"Well," I said, "I've been on my own in the wide world a lot longer than you have. And one thing I've learned is that there are some sounds that are far, far worse than car engines and rain."

Luck

"Hi!"

I was walking down the sidewalk in a funny little part of town I didn't know. The human houses seemed old at heart but they were newly cleaned and painted and defined. There were a lot of low wooden fences. And I was hailed from a front yard. I turned and saw a young male, black with white markings.

He came forward to where a gate stood open. "Hi," he said again. "How you doing?"

"Uh, fine," I said. "What's the problem?"

"No problem."

"Oh."

"Nice day, isn't it?"

It was and I said so, and then I wondered if he was one of those dogs who find it hard to talk about what's really on their minds. I said, "You hungry? Because I'm on my way to a restaurant three blocks from here. There's bound to be plenty of food out back."

"No," he said, "I'm not hungry."

"Oh."

"My name's Rorschach. What's yours?"

"I'm Rover."

"You live around here?"

"Just passing through."

"Really!" Rorschach said. "So your human is on the way from one house to another?"

"I don't have a human," I said.

"You don't? Oh, you poor dog."

I looked at him. Usually I'm a pretty good judge of age. Rorschach didn't look *that* young.

He said, "My human and I only moved in about a week ago, and I've been trying to get acquainted with the neighborhood dogs."

"Are there many around here?"

"Well, you're the third one who's passed by so far today."

"Passed by? Does that mean you don't go out?"

"My human doesn't like me to leave the yard."

I could see he had a collar, but there was no chain or rope and the gate was wide open. "You don't go out at all?"

"No."

"Because your owner doesn't like it?"

"That's right."

"What happens if you do go out? Does he kick you, or beat you?"

"Good heavens! Of course not!" Rorschach said. "He's not like that."

"Oh," I said. "So, what is he like?"

"He's great! He feeds me and he gives me milk, not just water. And I get regular baths, and I've got this great place to sleep—it's in the kitchen, next to an air-conditioning vent. Sometimes we go out for a run, and sometimes we just play. I've taught him this game where he throws a ball and when I bring it back, he throws it again in a different direction. He gets a real kick out of that. And sometimes at night, after we've been out, he just pats and hugs me, and I lick his face."

"Stop, stop!" I said, laughing.

"Oh," Rorschach said. "Okay."

"Now, tell me the real story."

"I don't know what you mean."

"So, what is it? He's all right, but his female is jealous?"

"He doesn't have a female," Rorschach said. "Well, not one who lives here. There's one female who came to stay in our last place now and then, and she's been to this one already. But sometimes there are others."

"And what do they do to you?"

"The females? Well, mostly they stroke my head and tickle my tummy. I *love* having my tummy tickled."

"But sometimes he forgets to feed you when he goes out, right?"

"Oh, never. In fact, usually he takes me with him, in his car. I really like it with the window open."

"That sounds dangerous."

"I don't think so," Rorschach said. "He puts a seat belt on me."

"But you must get lonely sometimes, right?"

"Well . . ."

"He goes away for a long time most days. Is that it?"

"Oh, no."

"No?"

"He works at home. He's got one of those jobs with a little TV screen. But he's never too busy to give me a pat or a scratch if I feel like it. All I have to do is go into his workroom."

"Oh," I said.

"Of course, at the house we lived in before he owned a female as well as me. Inky was her name. She was great."

"And what did he do to her?"

"What do you mean?"

"She's not here, right? I was wondering if maybe——"

"She was hit by a car," Rorschach said. "She didn't realize how dangerous they could be. She was young. A bit of an innocent, really."

"Oh."

"He cried and cried, my human," Rorschach said. "He held her body in his arms and he cried and——"

I held up a paw. "Stop. I get it now."

"Get what?"

"The bone has finally dropped. Oh, yes. Very good."

Rorschach looked uncertain.

"I went for it. I won't deny that. You got me. You got me good. Great. Most amusing."

"I don't know what you mean," Rorschach said.

"Come on! Enough's enough." I looked around. "So where are they? Behind the house?"

"Who?"

"The dogs who organized this little charade. You scammed me good. It doesn't happen often but you sure made a flea circus out of me."

"Rover, are you feeling all right?" Rorschach asked. "Why don't you sit down for a minute."

I looked around, but no dogs ran grinning like cats and, to tell the truth, it wasn't a very good place for a lot of dogs to hide. I sat. He couldn't be the real thing, could he? A dog who genuinely likes being his human's best friend. I spend so much time helping dogs cope or survive or escape, it was hard to believe.

Rorschach said, "Would you like to come in and have a drink of water? Oh, you said you were on your way to eat. Gosh, I've been so selfish! Not everyone is as lucky as I am. You don't have a human, so you must be starving. Come on. I'm sure my human will give you some food. He's very generous that way. Just the other day a cat came to the back door and as soon as my human realized it was thirsty he got out the cream and he——"

"Stop!" I said.

"Don't think of it as charity. Just think of it as one dog helping out another dog who's in trouble. I mean, if we can't help each other . . ."

"Stop, stop, stop."

Rorschach stopped.

"I'll be on my way now," I said.

"Or if you're sick, I'm certain my human would take you to the vet and get you fixed."

I jumped up. "Rorschach, it's been a pleasure meeting you."

"Well drop by again," he said as I trotted off.

But I would not be hurrying back to visit Rorschach in his open prison.

I know full well that few dogs thrive on the truly independent life. But, surely, even in a human household one can remain dog enough to tell the difference between an open gate and a closed one. There are so many wonders in the world.

"Anytime you're passing," Rorschach called after me. "I'll be here."

Creation

I WAS IN an alley when I heard a yelp that was half agony and half surprise. I left the garbage can I was working through and ran toward the call. "Where are you?" I shouted.

"Here. Help me, please!"

I followed the cry to a garage. The door was partly open. I ran in. And I found a tail. The dog connected to it was buried under a pile of newspaper, canvas, garden tools, and plastic netting. He, she, or it was thrashing wildly.

"Calm down," I said. "Calm down."

Immediately the dog stopped its struggling.

"Have you broken any bones?" I asked.

"I don't think so."

"Are you in pain?"

"No."

"Okay, keep still."

I cleared most of the junk easily and revealed a cream-colored male. It was harder to free his paws and one of his ears, all stuck in the plastic net, but finally I got him loose.

"Thank you," he said as he stood and shook himself. "For a while there I thought I was a goner. How embarrassing."

"What happened?"

He sat. "I was ripping a piece of plastic net when the shelf broke off the wall. I guess I panicked, because before I knew it I was entangled. I don't know what I would have done if you hadn't heard me."

"I'm glad I could help," I said, "but what did you want the piece of netting for? Is it good to eat?"

"Don't be silly," he said.

In the circumstances I didn't think it was me who "silly" applied to. I sat and had a good scratch. I'm sure my face said I was owed an explanation, but I didn't ask for it again.

After some thought the cream dog said, "You did save my life."

"Quite possibly."

"Can you keep a secret?"

"If it needs keeping. Why?"

"You look trustworthy," he said. "Come with me."

"Where?"

"To where I can explain."

Why not? "All right," I said.

"But first," he said, "help me tear off a piece of the plastic net, okay? My name's Arthur, by the way."

Severing threads of plastic was not what evolution had in mind for my teeth and I don't know how Arthur would have managed by himself. Nevertheless, we finally did it and set off on our way.

*   *   *

ARTHUR LED ME to a large, empty brick building. We went to the back and Arthur stopped at a boarded basement window. "You've got to promise not to tell," he said.

"Tell what?"

"I'll trust you," he said with an air of resolution. "Hold the plastic."

I held the plastic.

When he was satisfied that nobody was watching, he went to a piece of brick lying on the ground next to the window. He lifted it with his teeth. As he did so, the board on the basement window began to rise. I was so surprised I jumped back.

Arthur said, "Go in through the window. Move straight ahead but after four strides, stop and wait for me. Be quick. Once I put the brick down there's only five seconds before the board closes again."

I followed his instructions, and four seconds later he was standing behind me. A second after that we were in darkness.

"Just stay where you are," Arthur said. And he sprinted past me.

As I waited it gradually became light. Not bright, but light enough to see. Arthur trotted back and he was grinning like a mad thing. "It's an arrangement of my own invention," he said. "I use reflective surfaces. They gather sunshine in the day and streetlighting at night."

As my eyes adjusted I saw that the basement room was full of . . . things. "What is this place?" I asked.

"It used to be a school," he said. "And when I first moved in I found the *neatest* stuff tucked away here and there. Naturally I began to think about ways to use them."

"Use them how?"

"Well, to make my light gatherer," he said, "and . . . would you be interested in seeing my dog food can crusher?"

"Your what?"

"Step this way." He led. I followed. And he demonstrated a large, complicated device involving weights and pulleys that punctured the side of a dog food can and then crushed the contents out.

"Wow," I said.

He smelled the food. "Ah, fish flavor," he said. "My favorite. I'll save it for later. Unless you're hungry."

"Far be it from me to take food out of the mouth of the only dog I know who can open his own cans," I said.

"One day I hope to work out what the flavor is before I crush the can because I can't abide rabbit," he said. "But I've got about two hundred cans in stock. I'm sure that enough are edible that I could stay down here for a long time if I ever had to."

"Why would you have to?" I asked.

"There's a pack out there that hates me," he said.

"There is?"

"I've managed to keep out of their way for more than three years now, but when I was young, they decided to pick on me one day. I don't know why, but all five of them chased me and caught me and nearly killed me. After that I resolved it would never happen to me again. I found this place and . . . the rest is history."

I was about to say that packs rarely stay together more than a few months, much less three years, but then I looked around. The dark room was filled with exotic shapes and piles. "It's . . . astonishing here," I said.

"Of course the can crusher is merely practical," Arthur said. "Not like my best things. Come on."

He led me to the far end of the room where a stack of boxes

stood before a huge, puzzling structure. He climbed to the top of the boxes. "Watch," he said. He took a baseball from a box and dropped it into the bowl of a soup ladle that was hanging from a piece of wood.

The wood began to move and I saw that it was a lever. The weight of the baseball made the ladle end drop. As it did so, a bottle tied by string to the other end of the lever began to rise and swing. Then the ladle landed on some plastic guttering. The ball dropped out of the ladle into the guttering and ran down its length until it came to rest on the top of a cup. There the swinging bottle knocked the ball into a funnel which dropped it onto a pair of canes that acted like rails. The ball ran slowly down the rails until it dropped off the end and bounced away through the rest of the structure and onto the floor.

"See," Arthur said. "That's where I need a piece of plastic netting."

I didn't see at all, but I said, "Yes."

Arthur came down and joined me on the floor. "When I need something I don't already have, I look around outside. That's what I was doing today."

"So what's it all for?"

"For?"

"Yes. For."

"I don't think of it that way," he said. "When I get an idea of how this and that might fit together, I like to turn it into fact. It's satisfying to see it all working."

"I understand," I said. "I get satisfaction when something I think up works, though my efforts tend to be pretty practical."

"The funny thing," Arthur said, "it's often when I'm at work on one of my fanciful, blue-sky ideas that I get the inspiration for my most practical things."

"Like the can crusher?"

"Exactly. Though practical things can be beautiful too."

"Arthur," I said, "you are an amazing dog."

"I don't know about that," he said, sadly, "because I don't mix with other dogs. But I do wonder sometimes what I could accomplish if I didn't have aggressive packs to worry about, or dogcatchers, or the cats who sneak in here to make trouble. Speaking of which, my next idea is for a machine that will trap cats and then flick them out into a tree."

"A sort of catapult?"

"There's a large pine tree just outside a window upstairs. I'll need a lifting device to get them from the place I trap them to the flicking equipment." He thought for a minute, then nodded. "Yes. I ought to be able to do that." He looked at me. "But I wouldn't want to be cruel. Cats like trees, right?"

"Cats love trees," I said. I couldn't have sworn they feel the same about being hurled into pine needles, but I didn't say anything. I'd hate to dampen the creative process.

"Rover," Arthur said, "I'd like to show you the rest of my contrivances, but it will have to be another day. I'm getting restless, and if I don't get back to work soon I'll get sad."

"I'll leave you to it," I said. "If you'll tell me how to get out."

"Oh, right. Follow the central walkway to where we came in. Beneath the window there's a metal bar with red string wrapped around the end. Lean on that. The flap will open for five seconds. If you have any trouble, call me."

"I will," I said.

"And do come again another day. You'll want to see what I do with the netting. Just make sure no one's around when you open the flap."

"I will," I said, but Arthur was already climbing into his structure.

* * *

OUTSIDE, IN THE fresh air, I walked to the front of the empty school by way of a look at the pine tree. I sat for a while by the sidewalk. My admiration for Arthur's ingenuity was great, but so was my sorrow when I thought of him spending his life scrambling in the semidarkness of an abandoned school.

I wondered if I could convince him that the ferocious pack he was hiding from no longer existed. Probably not. It's hard to prove an absence.

Then, a thin human male turned the corner at the end of the block and ran my way. His running was labored, as if he had covered a long distance. But he wasn't chasing anything and nothing was chasing him.

I watched him approach, trying to understand the reason behind what he was doing. He lumbered past me, eyes never leaving the sidewalk in front of him. Could he possibly be enjoying his wheezy breathlessness?

Maybe he could. Maybe the human male's pouring sweat gave him the kind of satisfaction I get when I help a fellow dog and Arthur gets from making a beautiful contraption. I guess we all make up the point of our own existences.

I would never know for sure about the human male. So much of what his kind does seems pointless, and ugly, to me.

But Arthur, at least, could produce things of beauty. I got up and ambled away, pleased that one day I might be able to come back and see a pine tree decorated with startled cats.

Incarnation

I WAS IN a small park when the sun broke through the clouds
and a warm day threatened to become blazing hot. I'd just heard
about a supermarket that had thrown away a lot of cow and pig
and sheep. I wasn't particularly hungry, but you don't come
across nearly fresh meat every day so I was on the verge of setting out to see if the story was true. But the sudden sun made
me hesitate. I wasn't sure I wanted to leave the relative shelter
of a park for the heat trap of town streets. I could feel the temperature rise, and it wasn't long before I was hotter than I was
hungry.

The park contained a cluster of evergreen shrubs that was
perfect for passing the heat of the day. The shrubs were dense
and bushy on top but open underneath like a small cave. Unfor-

tunately, when I got to them I found three other dogs already en-sconced. Oh, well. "Room for another?" I asked.

"Sure," a small brown male said. The other two, a male and a female, said nothing. The silence was consent so I picked a place and settled myself.

"I'm Jock," the small male said. "This is Scamp and that's Kizzy-Koo. She hates her name."

"Big mouth," Kizzy-Koo said. "A big mouth always means a little—"

"My name's Rover," I said, interrupting.

"Brain," Kizzy-Koo said. "I was going to say a big mouth always means a little brain."

I asked, "Are you guys a pack?"

The second male, Scamp, said, "Not really. We live on the same street and run around together, but there's no leader, no initiation, no territory."

"Me?" Kizzy-Koo said. "In a pack with *him?*" Meaning Jock.

"Isn't it always the way?" Jock said. "You meet someone. You make puppies with her. And then she doesn't respect you after-ward."

"You two had a litter?" Scamp said. "I didn't know that."

"It was before you moved in," Jock said.

"I don't brag about it," Kizzy-Koo said.

"I do," Jock said. "I had to stand on a stone but I got there."

"At least it was an easy birth," Kizzy-Koo said. "They were all so *little.*"

"But tell them how many there were," Jock said.

"Felt like a hundred."

Scamp said, "You'd never guess it, Rover, but before you showed up we were talking metaphysics."

"We were?" Jock said.

"Life and death," Scamp said. "Whether there is life after we die."

"Oh," I said.

"Well what do you think, Rover?" Scamp said.

"I'm certain there will be life after I die," I said. "It just won't be mine."

"Well *I* believe in life after death," Jock said. "I believe in reincarnation."

Kizzy-Koo said, "What are you going to come back as next time? A dog for a change?"

"As you can see, Rover," Scamp said, "we maintain a high standard of wit around here."

"I'm sorry if I'm not witty enough for you," Kizzy-Koo said, "but it can't be a surprise. Anybody who would have a litter with *him* must be brain damaged."

"Next time I'd like to be . . . a cat," Jock said.

That surprised us all.

"Why?" Scamp said.

"Because they're so selfish. It must be nice not spend a single moment worrying what anybody else feels."

"There are dogs like that too," I said.

"Oh, I know," Jock said, "but for cats it comes naturally."

"You wouldn't want to be a human, then?" I said.

"Too savage," Jock said.

"If you believe in reincarnation," Scamp said, "then you must believe you had other lives before this one."

Jock hadn't thought about that.

"Your present being is just one stage in an infinity of incarnations, right?" Scamp said. "It didn't all begin with you, did it?"

"I guess not," Jock said.

"So what do you think you were before?" Scamp said.

Jock scratched and thought. But Kizzy-Koo said, "I've had lives before."

"You have?" Scamp said. He glanced at me. I shrugged. Neither of us knew whether she was serious.

She said, "My previous lives come back to me in dreams. I was a lot of dogs before the exquisite creature you see before you now."

"What lives have you had?" Scamp asked.

"Well, I was a Roman dog once," she said. "I clearly remember mountains and olive trees."

"Oh," Scamp said.

Kizzy-Koo looked at Jock. "Mountains are very *big*."

"Size isn't everything," Jock said.

"And more recently I was owned by a royal queen in a cool, wet country across a great sea."

"I'll take some of that coolth," Scamp said, "but hold the wet."

"I was a corgi," Kizzy-Koo said. "And my queen used to pick me up by the ears, but I didn't mind."

Jock was riveted.

"But the most fun," Kizzy-Koo said, "was being a pharaonic dog. I hunted with a human female princess that time."

"What did you hunt?" Jock asked.

"We hunted big, wild cats," Kizzy-Koo said. "Ten times as big as anything you see now."

"Wow," Jock said.

"I've met some of those Egyptian dogs," Scamp said. "And they have almost no voices at all. It's difficult to have a conversation with them, and they can't shout or sing or even bark."

"Ah, it was different back in my day. We had voices like anybody else."

"What happened to them?" Jock said.

"One day we decided that we'd already said everything there was to say," Kizzy-Koo said. "And so we didn't have to use our voices anymore, and eventually we lost them."

Jock was wide-eyed. "You'd said *everything* there was to say?"

"Everything worth saying," Kizzy-Koo said. "And sometimes I wonder if maybe we haven't reached the same point today."

She winked at me. "Witty enough for you, guys?"

Second Heat

IT WAS UNBEARABLY hot again, after a week of showers, breezes, relief. And something irritable came with the renewal of the heat. I could feel it in my body as if beamed down by the sun, a coursing, resentful edginess for no greater reason than that I could remember what it felt like to be cool.

I had experienced it in summers before. Other dogs did too. More than one scar on my body was the souvenir of a needless fight in a second heat. And if the restless fever was high among us dogs, the effect of the heat on human beings could only be imagined.

But I hate to accept bad things passively. I tried to respond to my bad mood and exercise it out. Despite the temperature, where normally I would have walked, I trotted. Where I would have trotted, I ran.

And I tried to wash it away, by drinking a lot of water.

And I did my best to keep completely to myself.

"Help!"

And I made it to the slight relief of night without trouble.

"Help! Help us, please!"

I was in one of those parts of town where the humans don't use the buildings they made.

"Pleeease!"

There are a lot of things you can do to avoid looking for trouble, but there's not much to be done when trouble looks for you.

THE DOG WAS calling from the highest window of a three-story house. The building was boarded up but there were holes in its walls. The dog was going crazy. With good reason. The house was on fire.

"How can I get up to you?" I shouted.

"There are stairs inside. Hurry! Hurry!"

There aren't many smells I like less than the smell of roasting dog. It's an odor I've experienced. I hurried.

The fire seemed confined to one side of the higher parts of the house. The stairs looked safe enough, and from where I was I couldn't see any reason why the dog in the window should have any difficulty escaping. Still, he would know better than I. I went up.

At the top of the stairs I saw the problem. The fire had eaten most of the hall floor. The dog could come to the doorway of the room he was in, but the only place to go from there was down, in flames. The jump to what remained of the landing at the top of the stairs was far too great.

Even so, when he saw me he shouted, "Here! We're here!"

I didn't see what I could do, other than shout that he should jump out the window and take his chances. Then suddenly part of the roof caved in above me.

I only just missed being hit by smoldering boards. But when I returned to the fiery gap between me and the trapped dog I had an idea.

I found the longest of the boards now lying on the stairs and pulled it up to the landing with my teeth. From there I pushed it toward the doorway the dog was standing in.

He understood what I was trying to do. He shouted, "When it gets close enough, I'll pull it in."

Only it never got close enough, because it was a couple of dogs too short to span the gap.

I pulled it back a bit and called, "Jump onto it. I'll weigh down this end so it doesn't give."

The dog looked at the fire below and hesitated.

"Do it now or I'm out of here!"

The dog withdrew into the room, but a moment later he reappeared like a furry rocket and jumped for the end of the plank.

He landed hard and nearly flipped me into the air. But he held his footing and I held mine and he scrambled to the landing and safety.

"Come on," I said. "Let's get out of here."

"No!" he said.

"What?"

"There's a cat in the room I just came from."

"So?"

"It's a living creature. We've got to help it if we can."

"It's a cat," I said. "It doesn't think of you as a living creature."

"That's what makes us different from them," the dog said.

I couldn't believe it. We were standing in a burning house and debating epistemology.

"Well, the plank's still there," I said. "If it wanted to be saved it would have used it already."

"It's in a corner, scared to death," the dog said. "And of course I didn't know how to explain to it."

"So what are we supposed to do?"

"I don't know!" the dog said pitifully. "But help it, please!"

It was the sort of decision you have only an instant to make. All day long I had sensed craziness in the air. I had tried to escape it. But there is no escape. Before I knew it I was risking my life for a cat.

The dog sat on the end of the plank. I sprinted its length and jumped into the isolated room.

Sure enough, there was a cat cowering in a corner. As soon as it saw me it hissed.

I don't speak cat, but I understand a hiss. It isn't friendly.

I've had cause to try to communicate with cats once or twice. I find that the only way to get through is to say what you have to say as loudly as you can. I've never had any success speaking quietly. Maybe it's some defect in their hearing. But what I screamed at this cat was, "If you don't want to become a catburger, then you better move your tail over to the door and jump for all you're catty worth, and do it now!"

After I screamed my message I moved toward the hissing feline pustule. I could feel the fire's heat under my paws. I knew I had no more than seconds to keep from becoming a dogburger myself.

Maybe the cat understood me, or maybe it had seen how we dogs left and entered through the door. Or maybe I just scared some of its lives out it. But before I got within snapping distance, the cat screeched and ran for the doorway and was gone.

I ran for the doorway myself. I had a terrible feeling that the dog I'd saved might not be on the other end of the plank. I jumped anyway. I had no choice.

But the dog, my fellow dog, was still there. I landed on the plank, and it rocked but held. And I scrambled to the top of the stairs. "Come on!" we said in unison, and we flew down those stairs and out the hole in the wall and didn't stop until the burning house was far behind and the hot air of the summer night felt cool to us.

"You saved my life," the dog said. "I don't know how to——"

"Stop," I said. "There is one thing I want from you now."

"What's that?"

"If you had anything whatever to do with that cat being in the house in the first place, I want you out of my sight, *now!*"

It was the kind of summer heat that could make a dog want to chase a cat into a house. It was the kind of summer heat that could provoke a dog to tear to bits someone whose life he'd just saved.

The dog stared into my eyes.

"Don't take a chance with me," I said. "I am *not* in the mood."

He rose and vanished silently into the blackness. So in a way, I'd saved the same dog's life twice in one night. It was that kind of heat.

Old Bones

I HADN'T SLEPT well, so my plan was to have a reasonable meal by the middle of the day and then find a quiet place in the shade where I could catch up on my z's.

The food part worked out well enough. I fed on scraps in an alley, and then, feeling an urge for something sweet, I slipped into the backyard of a big house where there were fruit trees.

Fruit is an acquired taste, but dogs who have been independent any length of time acquire quite a few tastes. I particularly like peaches. Maybe it's because they're furry. When I found several on the ground, I stuffed myself and was ready to sleep.

I was close to a schoolyard, and that's where I tucked myself into the shade made by a small shed and a large evergreen growing beside it. I was in dreamland moments after I stretched out.

Laughter woke me up.

The laughter was nearby and it was not friendly. I tried to ignore it and go back to sleep. But the aggressive hilarity and other loud talk continued, and it was no use.

I went out to take a look.

Just around the corner of the shed I found seven dogs. And they were so occupied with their own business that I was able to stand and watch without being noticed.

It didn't take long to understand what was happening. Six of the dogs were a pack. Together they were taunting the seventh, an old dog who had a bone. From where I stood the bone looked dry and tasteless, but the old guy was growling and bristling and he looked like he would take them all on, no matter what the consequences.

The pack leader was a muscular brown-and-white male of considerable size. The rest were smaller. The biggest of them was the youngest, barely out of puppyhood.

"You'll have to skin me first," the old dog snarled.

A brindled female made a listless lunge at the old dog's flank. But by the time the old guy had snapped at her, she was well out of range and chuckling.

"You see, Happy?" the leader said to the large young dog. "Any one of us alone might have trouble in a fight with this irritable old fella. But together, as a pack, nobody is in danger." The

young dog, it seemed, was being recruited for pack membership.

A gray male stepped forward next. He said to the old dog, "You want to be skinned? We can skin you as clean as your bone, can't we guys?"

The pack followers barked and laughed support.

The old dog snarled and spat.

The leader said to the young dog, "And suppose the old guy got lucky and hurt one of us. If you're injured and alone, you're vulnerable. There are some vile creatures in the world, Happy. Rats and cats, for example. They can smell blood, and they think nothing of attacking an injured dog while he's asleep. Think of it—half a dozen rats . . . No fun to fight them off if you're hurting."

Young Happy looked pretty dopey too. His eyes grew large as he visualized himself trying to fight off six enormous rats. He probably would have had trouble with one full-grown rat. Despite his size his every movement was young, loose, and soft. It can be a nice time in a dog's life. It can also be hell.

"But if you're part of a pack," the leader continued, "if you have me and the others to help you until you're fit again, to make sure you get enough food . . . Do you see what I'm saying, Happy?"

"I understand, Tarzan," Happy said.

"I was in a pack once," the old dog said. Everybody turned to look at him, surprised. "Yeah, I was. Worst time of my life."

"Can't have been a successful pack," Tarzan said with disdain.

"You think not?" the old dog said. "Well, the fact is we were the terror of the area. We went wherever we wanted. We did whatever we felt like. Leader was called Five Hundred. You ever hear of him?"

The pack followers turned to Tarzan. Tarzan said, "Never."

"Well, maybe you don't listen when other dogs talk to you.

Five Hundred led the biggest, meanest pack in this town, and I was a member and it was terrible. You want to know why it was terrible?"

The pack followers turned to Tarzan, who was clearly not inclined to pursue the subject. But dopey Happy said, "Why was it terrible?"

"Because it was an ugly way to live," the old guy said. "Everything about the pack was mean and nasty. Half the time we didn't eat what we killed, and that was despite there being so many of us, nearly twenty. We hunted and killed just for the fun of it. And then one day we killed a human child, and the pack got what it deserved."

The old dog cleared his throat and spat on the grass. He had everybody's full attention, and he knew it. He said, "The child we killed wasn't even one of the bad ones. But it's never smart to kill a child. Human beings don't tolerate that. So, do you know what they did?"

"What?" Happy asked immediately.

"Hunted down the whole pack," the old guy said. "And killed every last one."

"Gosh!" Happy said.

Tarzan rose and faced the old dog. "If they killed the whole pack, Pops, how come you're alive to tell the story?"

Once the pack followers understood his point, they all chimed in saying, "Yeah!" and "Why aren't you dead?" and "Ha!"

Tarzan turned to Happy and said, "You see a lot of this. Dogs who were never invited to join a pack bad-muzzling what they missed out on."

But the old dog was not intimidated. "You want to know why I'm still alive? I'll tell you. Because just before they killed the child a car ran over one of my back paws."

He held up a rear paw and, true enough, it was deformed. "But did Five Hundred and the others look after me until I was better? They did not. I could have been a cat for all they cared. Not one of them brought me so much as a scrap of meat. All that help-each-other stuff is pure guff, pup. It's all fairy tales."

Tarzan said, "You're the one telling fairy tales, Pops."

"No, he isn't," I said.

Everyone looked around to where I was standing. I moved out into the sun. "Well, well, well," Tarzan said. "What have we here?"

I walked forward slowly. I was not looking to fight. I said, "I saw Five Hundred and his pack. Everything the old guy says about them is true."

All of them looked at the old dog.

I said, "I don't remember this particular dog, but it was a huge pack and it's true that they killed a child and that the humans killed them all."

"Well, maybe it is true," Tarzan said, "but my pack isn't crazy like that."

I said, "There can be good packs. And there certainly are bad packs. But the thing they share is the pack mentality. A pack dog loses the right to think for itself. And that even applies to the leader. If you're top dog and your pack is restless you can end up doing stupid things just to make yourself look good. No dog who likes to think for itself could be content in a pack."

"And you never know whether the puppies are yours," the old dog said.

We all turned to look at the old guy, and we all started to laugh, even Tarzan. And the laughter completely took the danger out of the situation.

But the old dog didn't understand. "Well you don't," he said. "And that's important to some of us."

Tarzan sensed that he had lost the initiative. He said, "Come on. Let's leave these two to trade memories of the old days." And he set off across the schoolyard. The four grown-up pack followers trailed after him, but Happy hesitated, looking at the old dog's deformed paw.

I said, "What you have to think about, Happy, is why did Tarzan's pack taunt another *dog?* Aren't there better things to do?"

From a distance, Tarzan called, "We're going to get some fresh meat, Happy. Are you coming?"

Happy looked Tarzan's way and then ours. Without another word he ran after the pack.

"Natural-born follower," the old dog said. "To think for yourself you have to have a brain."

"Maybe when he's older," I said.

"Now you," the old dog said, "you bristle brains."

"Thanks."

"Does having so many brains make you stupid? Why'd you butt into this?"

"Dogs shouldn't pick on other dogs."

"I'd have been all right."

"By scaring them with tales of Five Hundred's pack?" The old dog chuckled. I said, "How did you hurt your paw?"

"Oh, it was a car all right. And not a single pack member ever brought me any meat."

"Especially not a member of Five Hundred's pack. Was there ever such a thing?"

"Made it clean up," he said, settling down on the grass. "But I did know a female called Five Hundred once. Lovely female, that one. I remembered her when was chewing on this old bone this morning and she just popped into my mind when I needed her. Invented the biggest meanest pack in history as a tribute."

"Was she mean?"

"Sweet and gentle," the old dog said. "Sweet and gentle."

"And I'll bet you knew whose her puppies were, right?"

Amenities

I WAS PASSING through a playground when I noticed a dog with a group of human children. The dog was that kind who's white but covered with black spots. The children were patting and feeding him, and I assumed one of them was his owner, but then the dog snapped at a child whose only mistake was to come up behind him.

The children jumped back, as a pack. The whole mood changed. One child picked up a twig and hit the dog on the head. It couldn't have hurt, but the dog snarled. Other children began to search the ground for sticks. One picked up a stone. I've seen it before, human children turning nasty quicker than a tail wag.

I shouted to the dog, "This way, this way!"

He lifted his head and saw me.

"Come on!" I called.

A child smacked him on the ear with its hand. But instead of giving the child some toothmarks to remember him by, the spotted dog dodged away and ran in my direction. Together we soon left the baying pack far behind. There's hardly anything more evil than human children in the wrong mood, but they're not quick.

When we were alone I asked the spotted dog, "What was that all about?"

"The smelly one hit me," he said.

"No, before that," I said. "When you snapped at the one who came up behind you."

"Did I?" he said, but it wasn't by way of denying it.

"Don't you remember?"

"Not specifically, but I wouldn't be surprised. I'm a little jumpy these days."

"Why's that?"

"I'm not used to being in a town. Nothing here feels right. I grew up on a farm. You know, catching rats and that whole thing. Oh, I could just do with some rat right now. I've got a real hankering."

"There are plenty of rats in a town if that's what you need to make you feel better," I said.

"Are there?" The spotted dog brightened like the sun coming out from behind a cloud.

So there I was, having promised to find him some rats.

THE ONLY PLACE you can count on for rats is the dump. But the dump is dangerous. Human beings may leave their waste all over town without a second thought but in the one place where it's actually stored, they make a show of caring. And among the things they do there is sweep through to capture stray dogs.

Teams of human beings use nets and long sticks with choking loops at the end. It doesn't happen often, but I've never met a dog who was captured at the dump and came back to tell the tale.

The dump has its upside. There's always plenty of food out there and you never need to chase anything with a tail and teeth. But every dog who knows how to mark a streetlight knows the dump is not a place to eat regularly, unless you're desperate. However, if you need a rat and need it fast, it's perfect.

The spotted dog's name was Ralph, and he hadn't been on his own long. When he was born he was owned by a human being who bred a few spotted dogs as well as farming. But one day Ralph was out catching rats, and when he returned to the house, the human being and his family were gone and so were all the other dogs.

Ralph stayed put for a week, trying to work out what had happened. But when no one came back he set out to find some of his family. Given the generations who'd been born on the farm, he was confident that he'd find someone.

He'd found me. And I was taking him to the dump.

THE DUMP IS huge. The tastiest things are where the trucks drop fresh loads, but if you're not fussy there's food everywhere. Rats are not fussy. They're everywhere too. Ralph was in ratters' heaven. As soon as we were under the fence, we saw two.

Ralph relaxed before my eyes. "Thanks a million, Rover," he said. "I would have gone crazy back in town."

"Just remember not to stay too long."

"I'll remember." He ran off before I could say, "Catch one for me." The dump rats were in for a shock. Not many dogs as young and fit as Ralph spend time here.

I considered chasing down a rat or two myself. They're not my favorite meal, but fresh meat has a lot to recommend it.

Then I was startled by a voice behind me. It said, "Hello, Rover."

I turned aggressively, but what I saw was an old, sick female. She had open sores on her legs and patches of hairless skin. She had lost teeth.

"Don't bite my head off," she said submissively. "I only said hello."

"Sorry, you surprised me. But how do you know my name?"

"Don't you recognize me?"

I didn't. I said, "No."

"Tsk tsk. And they say dogs always remember their first."

I stared.

"Still, in those days you probably told all the females they were your first."

"Poppy?"

"You *do* remember," she said, obviously pleased. She sat, carefully. "I guess I have changed a lot."

Is night different from day? "No, no," I lied. "It's just that you're the last dog in the world I was expecting to meet out here."

She shrugged. "I'm not as strong as I used to be." Then, with what I think she intended to be a lascivious grin, she said, "But I bet you are."

"I thought you had a permanent home with a human being who had a store."

"So did I," she said.

"It wasn't . . . me, was it?"

"You? Oh, you mean your puppies? No. It was a long time after that."

"My puppies?"

"Two males and a female. And fine, healthy dogs, all of them."

"That's nice to know." I felt a moment of sadness that I'd never seen them.

"But the world must be full of your puppies by now," Poppy said. "What a strong, handsome dog you are. Not that you weren't then, young as you were."

"I was certainly young."

"You don't think I was litter-snatching, do you?"

"No, Poppy," I said truthfully. "You were a young dog's dream. I was lucky and privileged."

"Good." She looked dreamy. "Oh, it was such a long time ago."

"It is wonderful to see you again."

"Well, now you know where I am," she said with a sigh.

And I could tell that she understood exactly what the dangers were. Not just the human beings and their occasional cleanups. The dump rats don't let sleeping dogs lie. Not a sleeping dog whose hearing is maybe not what it was back when she was young and the most alluring creature imaginable.

"Poppy," I said, "is there anything I can do to help you?"

She laughed at me. "What are you suggesting, Rover? That you'll stay here with me?"

"No," I agreed.

"But I am glad I got to see you again," she said. "It's good to know that, at least once, I picked well." She struggled to her feet and turned to go.

"Hang on," I said.

"What?"

"If you see a spotted dog called Ralph, tell him you know me. He owes me a favor."

She nodded.

I went to her. I licked the sores on her legs. Then I dug her a safe little lair and caught her half a dozen rats.

Maybe some rest and fresh meat would let her roll back a few minutes of all those years. And maybe Ralph would feel like some company. He might even stay around long enough to make sure that it wasn't the rats that got her.

Communication

SOMETIMES YOU JUST know. A female appears behind you, and before you see her you know she's there and that you want her and that she wants you. It's exciting when it happens, and sweet.

"Oh, wow," I said when I turned around. My tongue was hanging out. I must have looked like a fool.

But she didn't seem to mind. She said, "Hi."

"Hi."

"Going my way?"

"To the end of the earth if that's what it takes."

"The park is closer."

While we waited to cross a street I asked her name.

"Lassie. But don't you dare say a thing."

156

"How could I? I'm Rover."

We laughed all the way into the park. When it hits you like that, everything is funny.

And we had a real good time.

"Oh, Dog," she said. "I think I'm in heaven."

"In that case the park's been moved."

"I felt it happen."

"Me too."

The afternoon was delicious.

WHEN THE SUN began to set, Lassie felt hungry and decided to go home. Before she left she said, "If how they are made matters, this is going to be a litter of superdogs."

We parted as good, good friends.

As she waited to cross the street I heard her say, "I went with someone called Rover?"

I watched her until she was out of sight. I was more tired than hungry so I went back into the park. I found a bush and lay down beside it and watched the sunset sky.

* * *

WHEN I WOKE up, it was deep night but with a bright moon. However, it wasn't the moonlight that woke me. It was the screams.

Not far away something was afraid. It wasn't a dog, but it didn't sound like an owl or a cat either. I heard commotion in the undergrowth. Maybe something was being pursued for food.

The thought of food made me realize I was hungry now. What I felt like was some pizza. And I knew of a pizza restaurant that wasn't far. Being owned may have the advantage of two full bowls a day without hassle, but what happens when you get a particular taste in mind? When I hear of a human being that offers a menu maybe I'll consider giving myself up to a collar.

The noise nearby continued. The fearful screams had given way to painful cries, so whatever was doing the killing was doing it badly. The racket began to annoy me so I decided to see if I could sort the ruckus out.

However, what I found was not a hunt for food. In a clearing a human male was on top of a human female. His pants were in a pile by his feet, and what he was trying to do to her was obvious. But it was equally obvious that she was not in the mood, so it hurt and she was screaming.

I will never understand human beings. What is the point of trying to do it with a female when she doesn't want to? With us no means no. No hard feelings. Maybe some other time. What was happening here looked more like a fight, a one-sided fight at that.

Of course, it was not my problem—it was the human female's. Yet I felt the impulse to get involved. Maybe it was because of what I had shared with Lassie in that very park.

So I ran to the human male and shouted in his ear. "Stop it, you deranged piece of rotting meat. She doesn't want to. Even an ancient tomcat with no sense of smell could tell that. Why can't you? Are you deaf, dumb, and blind? If it's just a fight you're after, you can fight me."

And I bit the male on his rump.

To tell the truth, I'd never bitten a human except through its clothes. I hadn't expected my teeth to sink in quite so far. But I didn't rip a chunk off. It was pizza that I wanted. I just let him go.

And he sure let her go. He jumped off and howled even louder than she had.

I squared up for another nip but the male backed away from me. At the same time the female scrambled into some bushes. But I couldn't check if she was all right because the male had found a stick. He ran toward me waving it.

Sometimes a human being with a stick wants to play. But this was a male in a fighting mood, and he intended to use the stick to do me harm—no creature-to-creature fair fight for him.

Well, if he wanted to fight dirty I could too. I picked up his pants and ran away a few steps.

I don't see the big deal about pants myself, but I know that human beings value them, almost above all other things. And when this male saw what I'd done he screeched something in-comprehensible and threw his stick at me.

The stick wasn't close to hitting me, so maybe he expected me to drop his pants and fetch it. Instead I ran a few more steps. The male chased after me. Then he found a stone. He threw that at me. I backed off. And then we did it all again. I wanted him out of the park and well away from the female, and it wasn't hard to get him there.

Once I got to the street I took the male's pants to the gutter and dropped them. And I left.

I had gone only a few steps when I heard the male dash out of the shrubbery to retrieve his precious pants. I turned on him. For a moment he froze. I lunged at his ankle. And I got it.

The male dropped onto the sidewalk like the excrement he was. He grabbed his ankle and howled. I stayed with him, shouting in his ear, until I saw a passing car slow down. I picked up the male's pants and ran back into the park. Let the male explain himself to other human beings if he could.

I FOUND THE female huddled beneath a tree. She was whimpering, but when she saw me she stopped. She extended a hand and said things I didn't understand, but I knew they were friendly.

I dropped the pants beside her. If pants had power, perhaps she could draw on it. But instead of picking up the pants she patted my head and hugged me and pulled me close. And all right,

I admit, I licked her face. It was the first time I had done *that* to a human being in a long time.

This one was salty. It made me wonder if they come in different flavors.

Then, at last, the female let me go. She picked up the pants, but she didn't put them on. She looked through the pockets and found things that seemed to please her. Well, whatever.

Then she stood and began to walk out of the park. I walked with her as far as the sidewalk. The male was not in sight, so I left her. No point in dragging out good-byes.

Not when you're famished and crave pizza.

The Mongrel Next Door

As I was ambling down an alley, the very last thing on my mind was love. In fact I was in pain, following a small contretemps with a child on a bike.

It was caused by a pizza. That may sound absurd but in the morning I found half a pepperoni pizza thrown out in its box. Unfortunately I wasn't alone when I found it and as I was about to see off my would-be breakfast companion, a child rode by on a bicycle. Inadvertently I stuck my tail in the spokes.

What a shock! No lasting harm done, but it stung like mad. No pizza is worth that. I left it to the other dog. At that particular moment I'd have given it up to a cat.

So there I was, making slow progress to nowhere special and stopping to lick my wound every few minutes. And then, on a summer breeze, I caught a whiff of perfume. And I was in love.

* * *

SHE WAS BIG and shaggy and beautiful. But she was an owned dog and locked in a backyard pen made of wire fencing against a garage wall. She had her own house built against the garage, so I guessed she was comfortable and well enough cared for. But a guess isn't a fact. Maybe she was unhappy. Maybe she wanted to see a bit of the outside world. I could see right away that the fence would be a problem. But if love is tricky on the one paw, it is determined on the other. An obstacle or two can make it sweeter. I went up to the wire to say hello.

"Hi there, beautiful," I said.

"Oh, Dog," she said. "Not another one."

"That's not very friendly."

"I don't mean to be friendly." Then she called out, "Wooffitt! Wooffitt!"

Immediately I heard movement nearby. A voice shouted, "I'm coming!"

"Hey, what's the big deal?" I said.

"You'll see," she growled.

And I did. In a matter of seconds a big male crashed through a row of shrubs that separated the property next door from that of female's owner. "Get away from her!" the big male snarled at me.

With the female inside the wire fence and me outside, I didn't see any urgency in the situation. But the angry male gave every evidence of being ready to tear me to shreds. "Go on. Get away! She's mine."

However, possession, like love, can be hard to establish and the very devil to maintain. I faced him. "Keep cool, cousin. Don't bite off more than you can chew."

"I told you to go away!" he shouted again.

And that established he was not a fighter, no matter how much racket he made. True fighters don't issue warnings twice.

So maybe he was a lover, like me. I said, "When it comes to the company she keeps, I'd have thought that it was up to the female to speak for herself." But at that the female began to cry.

It was the last thing I expected. When I turned to look, the big male could have done me real damage. What he did instead was push past me and stick his snout through the fence and nuzzle her. "There, there, Dominique," he said.

"I'm so miserable, Wooffitt," she said.

DOMINIQUE'S STORY WAS a sad one. Pedigreed dogs can be arrogant when it comes to hoi polloi, but not Dominique. She and this mongrel next door had been close friends for a very long time.

Most of the year they hung around together with no problems. But when it came to the season of love, Dominique's owner locked her in the pen. He never let her out alone and, of course, he never let Wooffitt in.

A dog who gets around at all will have heard stories like this before, but that did not make their situation any the less sad. And I got to thinking that it would be nice to find a way to help the lovers. To tell the truth, it was also nice to have something to take my mind off my tail. So I left them together and checked out the pen.

The fence was high, too high. And the wire was heavy gauge and not rusty and anchored in concrete. At each end the fencing was firmly fixed to the garage. The gate to the pen was secure. Things did not look promising.

I went away to get some food and to think.

*   *   *

WHEN I GOT back the lights in Dominique's owner's house were out. I found that Wooffitt had saved some of his canned food for me. "That's a generous gesture," I told him, "but you better eat it. You're going to need your strength."

I showed him what I had in mind.

The wire fence was still hopeless. But Dominique's pen had a fourth side, the garage, and the garage was old. The floor inside it was solid, but I figured there was a chance that we could claw through part of the wall. How good a chance was hard to tell. One can but try.

WOOFFITT AND I took turns and scratched until our claws ached. On her side Dominique scratched too but also kept watch for her owner. We worked most of the night, and at long last we got through. The hole we made led directly into Dominique's doghouse.

I left it to the lovers to decide how best to use it. Dominique might choose to come out and hit the road with Wooffitt. The independent life is not for everyone, but two is safer than one, and the fact they got along is no small thing. However raising puppies out in the big wide world isn't easy and should not be undertaken lightly.

An alternative was to cover the hole in the garage wall when they weren't using it. There was plenty of junk lying around that would do the job. If they were careful, they could come and go as they pleased. The only immediate risk was a garage sale. Not ideal, perhaps, but then how much of life is full water bowls and shag rugs by the fireside?

The longer-term problem was what would happen when

Dominique's human saw her puppies. He might just put another two feet of wire fencing on top of what was already there. Or he might search for the hole and patch it.

Or maybe he would be more farsighted. Wasn't the point of creating pedigrees to save special and desirable canine characteristics? Maybe Dominique's owner would think the offspring of a mongrel who'd created a tunnel of love to be worth encouraging.

Still, what Dominique and Wooffitt decided to do was their business. When the sun was on its way up, I knew it was time for me to go. If I stayed around I might lose control. There really are only so many times you can call a grown dog Wooffitt without laughing, and I would have hated to cause offense.

Chaser

THE DOG SHOUTED as he ran. "It's a good thing you're rolling, you slime on wheels, because if you stop you won't see tomorrow! I'll tear your rubber into play bones! I'll rip your seats into lining material for my doghouse! When I'm done nobody will recognize you! Not even the creatures that assembled you in the first place could make you roll again!"

The dog was pursuing a car that had three human beings inside. I followed to give support.

To make my position crystal clear I called out, "And anything my species colleague promises to do to you goes double for me!" But it wasn't long before the car was well away and the shouting dog had stopped running after it.

"Hey," I said as I drew near, "what did they do to you?"

"Do to me?" he asked. "They didn't do anything to me."

His response puzzled me. I'm not shy about shouting at human beings. There's rarely a shortage of just causes. But I still don't do it without a reason.

"My name's Monty," the shouting dog said. "I'm heading back home now. Come along."

I FOLLOWED MONTY to a large house, and he lay down under a tree in front of it. It was a pleasant enough day and I wasn't on my way to anywhere in particular, so I stretched out near him and chewed on the grass and waited for Monty to explain.

But Monty didn't have much to say. He acted as if what had taken place was as natural as the butterflies.

Then, suddenly, he sat up.

I didn't hear anything special. Just a car in the street.

Monty ran down to the sidewalk. As the car approached, he stepped off the curb. And as the car came level with him, he began to shout at it.

"If you dare stop here I'll show you what's what, you bellowing box of steel!" He ran alongside the car. "Come on, stop!

I dare you! See what happens! I'll make your tires into rubber bands before you can say Rin Tin Tin! The mat in your trunk will be in shreds so fine that the birds will use them for nesting! Hey, where you going! No guts? Come on, stop! Stop now! I double-dare you!"

The driver of the car had glanced down when Monty appeared. She accelerated as she passed him.

When the vehicle was well down the road Monty turned to trot back to his tree.

He lay down.

"Monty, why did you do that?" I asked him.

"Do what?"

"Chase that car."

"Did I?" He glanced toward the street. "Oh. I suppose I did."

"You can get hurt chasing cars," I said.

"I know." He held up his left front paw. Two of the claws hung oddly. "Green one three weeks ago. I got too close."

"But why do you do it, Monty?"

He looked at the street again, then turned back to me. There was an odd expression on his face, partly wistful yet with a darker element too. He said, "There's something about cars. They drive me *wild*."

As if to underline the point two cars passed the house one after the other. Monty's rage at them surpassed anything I'd heard for the cars that had passed alone.

Afterward, he came back to his tree.

I waited.

He licked his damaged paw. He said, "I know it's dangerous. I know it's pointless. But when I do it, when I've done it, I just feel better. It's something inside me. A feeling I get between my legs. I chase a car and I feel I've *done* something. For a moment I feel fulfilled."

We lay quiet. I looked up at the clouds, all chasing each other. I said, "How do you feel when a car hits you?"

"Stupid, of course."

"Do you remember when it all started?"

He looked reflective. "You know, I've never thought about it. It's like eating and drinking and making puppies whenever I get the chance. It's something I do. I can't remember not chasing cars."

"In the beginning, did you do it with somebody else?"

Monty was silent as he considered this. A car drove by the house and, although he watched it closely and his ears twitched, he stayed where he was in the grass.

He said, "I don't have to do it, you know. I can take it or leave it."

"I asked if you used to do it with anybody else."

"Yeah," he said quietly. "Mom was a chaser. I don't think about it very often, but I started chasing with her."

"Here?"

He nodded. "I've always lived here."

"Did your brothers and sisters chase?"

"I was an only pup," Monty said.

"It's nice you got to know your mother."

"Yeah," he said, and he had a good scratch.

I said nothing.

"She died, when I was still pretty young."

"How?"

"Car."

"Oh."

"Yes, yes," he said sharply. "Your potted psychology is right on target. She was killed here in the street. Yes I was with her. Yes we were chasing. But she slipped and she went under a back wheel and that was that."

"I'm sorry," I said.

We were silent for a few minutes more.

Then, as they will, a car approached.

Monty hesitated, but then he jumped up and ran out to it. His invective was louder and fiercer than anything I had heard from him before. "You foul, murdering, scabrous . . ."

When the car was gone he stood in the street looking after it. He turned toward the house, but he walked slowly.

I stood and went to meet him.

Before I could say anything he said, "I know it's dopey, but I get a sensation of power when I chase them. I chase and they run. I've made it happen. For just a moment it feels better than anything else could."

Anything except changing the past. I raised a paw and clenched it. "More power to you, Monty," I said and trotted away.

Nature's Way

IT WAS A warm, humid day. I was in a part of town where the houses are large, and I was looking for cat food.

Although I've been independent most of my life, when I was born I was owned. My first solid food came from a can. And although my years and experiences have moved me a long way from puppyhood, sometimes I get a powerful urge to taste canned food again.

What set me off this time was the smell of wet wool. Suddenly I was back with my mother and my brothers, and we were in the basket we shared during my first few months alive. Those were wonderful, innocent, ignorant days. All the world was new and fun. Nothing was bad.

I live in a very different kind of world now but when the

puppyish craving hits me I try to satisfy it. It's a gesture of respect to the past.

What I do is find a part of town where the human houses are big. The bigger a house is, the more likely the humans inside are to keep "pets." And where there are pets there is canned pet food.

I wouldn't take what belonged to another dog, no matter how pampered. But cat food is something else entirely. It might not taste like the canned food I remember, but nothing now could ever be that exciting and exotic. A bowl of canned cat food satisfies my nursery needs just fine.

THE BIG HOUSES I found this day had large yards and a lot of trees. I didn't pick up cat scent at once. Instead the first thing of interest that I found was a pond with fish in it. I watched the fish swim for a while. I wondered if human beings thought of fish as "pets" too?

It occurred to me that the reason that a few human beings live in relative isolation in these big houses might be that something's seriously wrong with them. Perhaps they're not allowed a closer association with "normal" human beings. Maybe these extra-damaged ones get lonely and that's why they keep pets. For warmth, affection, and good company dogs would be the obvious choice. So maybe it's only the badly flawed humans who find ways to gain satisfaction by keeping cats, and fish.

These particular fish were small and quick as they swam in and out among their weeds. On another day I might well have dipped my nose in the water and snapped at a couple of them. I've always figured I could catch a fish that way if I really tried.

But I had cat food in mind, not fish food. I got up and walked to the grounds of the next house. There I immediately smelled cat. And I smelled cat food. Liver flavor, to be precise.

Cautiously, I prowled around the house checking for signs of the presence of humans, like cars in the driveway or movement in the windows. Nothing. So I followed the liver scent to the garage.

Human beings don't have sensitive noses so they think no one else does either—which is human reasoning in a nutshell. They think if they leave food out sight it's safe, even though they've left enough space under the garage door for an agile dog to crawl in.

Which is exactly what I did. And I cleaned a bowl of its chunky liver. Craving satisfied. And there was a bowl of water to wash it down with. Perfect. Over to you, kitty.

When I slid back out under the door, I saw the kitty in question. He—or she, who can tell with cats?—was jumping in the grass. At first I thought it was playing some demented feline game, but as I got closer I saw that the object of this cat's attention was no ball or stick. It was a young rabbit.

Nature's way. Dog eats cat food. Cat eats young rabbit.

But as I watched I saw that the cat was doing nothing of the kind. The cat *was* playing a game. It would catch the young rabbit, pin it down with claws and teeth, and then it would let the poor thing go. The bunny would jump up squealing, and it would run. The cat would catch it and start again.

I've seen this kind of thing before but I've never understood why cats do it. If they'd rather eat their canned cat food than warm bunny, why hunt the bunny in the first place? And having caught one, why torture it? Does having some poor young rabbit at its mercy make a cat feel big? That's about as juvenile an attitude as you can get.

The bunny was screaming. I approached the cat from behind, quietly. I waited for the stage in its cycle of torture when it dropped the pleading rabbit yet again. I ran at the cat shouting, "You are pathetic, kitty. You are a miserable excuse for a creature. Grow up!"

The cat turned to look at me. It didn't comprehend a word, but it had sufficient low cunning to understand that I meant it no good.

It glanced at the bunny. I could tell that the cat was wondering whether to try to carry the bunny as it got away from me. But the cat played it safe and left the young rabbit as it ran for the nearest tree.

Good decision.

I paused when I got to the cat's victim. It lay in the grass, and its frozen eyes made me think that I'd arrived too late. But then its nose twitched.

"Go on," I said. "Get yourself out of here."

The nose twitched again, and then the bunny jumped up and ran, shrieking, into nearby shrubbery. It didn't thank me.

I turned back to the cat. It stood at the base of the tree, staring at me. I understand enough of the feline character to know that if I left it now the cat would chase after the rabbit again. And, being inherently perverse, it would probably enjoy the hunt all the more for the interruption.

I ran at the cat. I shouted, "Please stay right where you are, kitty. Make my day."

But the cat jumped onto the tree and raced up the trunk.

"Aw, kitty," I called, "don't you want to play with me? I thought you liked games."

It scrambled onto a branch above me, out of my reach. It glowered and hissed.

I sat down and had a good scratch. "Kitty," I said, "I just don't get the point of making an animal suffer before you kill it. Any dog that caught a rabbit would put it out of its misery with one quick snap. Unless maybe it was a puppy."

The cat said something that sounded like, "Yeeeooow!"

"Is that what it's all about?" I said. "Do you behave in an infantile way because, being owned, you've never been allowed to grow up?"

"Ssssssrrrow!"

"Being owned you don't have to hunt to eat. There's always food waiting when you want it, like there was from your mother when you were a tiny kitten. So maybe you never learned that food is something serious."

"Miurrrreowyowyow!"

At that moment a car roared into the driveway of the big house. I said, "Kitty, I'd love to continue exploring the origins of your stunted, immature behavior, but I think your owner might not realize that we're having a civilized psychological discussion."

"Yeurrrrowssss!"

"My advice, kitty," I called, "based on years of hard-won wisdom, is that you should leave these flawed human beings to their own company and feed yourself. It's your only chance to achieve a little maturity. And to help you get started, I've disposed of the cat food food in the garage. No need to thank me."

"Ruowowowsss!"

A door on the car slammed.

"Sorry, kitty, but I've got to run." And I did, feeling about as pleased with myself as I get. A good day.

Tail

IT WAS NOT a good day. It started with the sun being too hot. Then a female was too cold. And finally I went to sleep hungry. Not a good day.

Being hungry was the worst part. Some days every plastic bag you check has tasty morsels inside and you're spoiled for choice. But occasionally you find nothing but paper and old shoes and broken electrical equipment. In a whole alley—and we're talking four blocks here—all I found that was worth eating was half a cheese sandwich.

So I ate it and gave up. I lay down under a bush and decided to get to tomorrow as fast as I could. It would have to be better than today. What I didn't realize was that today wasn't finished with me yet.

What happened was that I had a dream. In it I was chasing my tail, the way I used to when I was a pup and my tail was a tantalizing, mysterious thing that flicked out of sight just as I twisted my neck around far enough to see it. My tail was always running away from me and so I had to chase it, and chase it, and chase it. And then I woke up. I was exhausted.

It was still deep night and dark. I considered getting up to look for food, but I was too tired. So I scratched behind an ear and curled up again.

And this time I dreamed I was chasing a rabbit. And I caught it, only it looked up at me with such pathetic puppy eyes that I didn't have the heart to kill it and eat it.

But then my mother appeared behind me. She said, "Aren't you hungry, Rover?" She was huge and shaggy and had fierce yellow eyes—not at all the way she looked when she was alive. But I knew it was her.

My mother was frowning. "A rabbit is game, not a game," she said. "Dogs aren't cats. Dogs chase to eat."

But when I looked back at the rabbit it hopped behind me, and as it did it turned into a toad, an evil-smelling, slimy toad.

"See?" my mother said. "You had your chance but you wasted it. You can't eat a toad. You'll poison yourself."

"No I won't," I said. And I snapped at the toad, but then my tail began to hurt. I twisted my neck around to see what was happening but I couldn't twist far enough. Round and round and round I went but I couldn't catch sight of my tail.

"Oh, Rover," my mother said, and the tone of her voice made it clear that I never did anything right and I was a disappointment to her.

Then I woke up. My tail was in my mouth. It was the dream. A rabbit with puppy eyes. A toad who made my tail hurt. Worst of all, the feeling that my mother didn't like me anymore. Even though she was dead. I felt miserable.

I stood up. I stretched and had a scratch. I gave myself a good shake, but I couldn't shake off the dream. The only part of my discomfort that I felt I could do something about was being hungry. So I headed toward the center of town.

IN BACK OF some small houses I found a torn plastic bag that smelled of meat. I ripped it open and found some sausages that were beginning to rot. Normally I wouldn't have touched them, but they felt about right for a dog whose mother didn't like him anymore.

A voice from behind me said, "I'm surprised at you, Rover."

For an instant I thought it was my mother again. I jumped around but the voice came from a small female named Colleen.

"What's the matter? Cat got your nose?" Colleen said. "Those sausages are so old they're growing whiskers."

"They'll do," I said.

"No they won't. They'll make you sick."

"What's with you females? All of a sudden everything I want to eat will make me sick." I took a big mouthful of the sausages. The taste was horrible. I spat it out.

Colleen nuzzled me. "It isn't like you to poison yourself on rotten meat, Rover. And it isn't like you to greet me without a sniff or a wag. What's the matter?"

Colleen and I have been friends ever since we had a little fling near the river. I knew she deserved better from me. "I'm out of sorts, that's all," I said.

"Bad hair day?"

"More a bad hare day." I told her about my dream.

"So *that's* why you were eating poison," she said when I had finished. "You thought that if you sicked up what was in your belly you could clear out what's on your mind."

"Oh yeah?" I said. "What cat's entrails did you read that one in?"

"Young-Joy told me," Colleen said. "She said a lot of dogs make that mistake, especially males. You think you can cure the mind through the belly.

"Well, how *do* you cure the mind?"

"Not by eating moldy sausages," Colleen said. "But why don't you ask Young-Joy yourself? She's the wisest dog I know."

Young-Joy is one of those dogs we've all heard about, but Colleen was the first I ever knew who'd met her. Dogs with big reps are something of a problem for me. I admire genuine accomplishment but I've been disappointed so many times that nowadays I suspend judgment until I've met them myself. There's no shortage of stories about Young-Joy—that she's part wolf, that she has a wonderful memory, even that she considers herself to be the keeper of the independent dogs' "pack" archive, whatever that is. I always figured it meant she was a gossip.

But the fact of the matter is that Young-Joy has been around for a lot longer than I have, and that is no small accomplishment for an independent dog. So maybe Young-Joy *was* special.

"Okay," I said. "I will ask her myself. Where do I find her?"

"You don't just 'find' Young-Joy," Colleen said. "You have to search her out."

"Oh, great," I said. "Hassle. Just what I need today."

My rule has always been, if you want help, help yourself. I was getting what I deserved for being ready to break it.

But Colleen said, "Young-Joy and her friends were in the big park south of the river night before last. She moves pretty slowly these days, so they won't be far from there now. But she's worth the search, Rover. She really is."

And suddenly I felt a little better. The dream was still with me, but the idea of spending the day looking for Young-Joy gave me my first hint of relief. A search was much more my type of problem solving than finding a way to regain the approval of my dead mother. Let the old, wise wolf have the first crack at that one.

However, by the time the sun was setting I'd learned that finding Young-Joy was easier decided than done. I went to the park south of the river and asked every dog I saw. There were plenty of rumors and suggestions but no sightings. I didn't even come across another dog who'd ever met Young-Joy, although several said they knew someone who she'd helped. Like I did.

The moon came up early, before the sun had quite disappeared, and it hung like a giant bubble in the darkening sky. My paws were sore from nonstop padding around. I stopped to lick them, and as I did I heard a female start to sing. "Oh mother moon," the female sang, "give us light to hunt by, shadow to court in, hear our tune."

The sound came from a long way away, but it was clear. The female's voice was high and melodic and it made the hair on my back twitch. I was going to reply but before I could, a chorus of female voices joined the first singer. "Moon, moon, hear our tune," they sang. I got up and followed the song.

And that was how I found Young-Joy.

SHE WAS ON the open top floor of a high-rise parking lot. The moment I came onto the roof I found myself surrounded by about a dozen bristling females.

"Who are you?" one asked.

"What do you want?"

"State your business."

They weren't threatening a fight but they weren't friendly either. I sat down and said, "My name is Rover. I've been looking for Young-Joy since early this morning and my business is between me and her."

"Have you made an appointment?" one female said.

"Have you brought a present? She doesn't take charity cases."

"She's tired," another chimed in. "Come back some other time."

But before I could respond a cracked growl from outside the ring said, "Pipe down, you lot. Let me see this Rover."

Young-Joy was a grizzled female of great size and weight. She was so old that her ruff was nearly white. Her teeth were yellow and blunted. But her eyes were golden-brown and they gleamed as they took me in.

"And is that what you are?" she said. "A rover?"

"I get around," I said. "And I've done miles today trying to find you." I lifted one of my tender paws. "Swollen, see?"

"The road *should* be long," Young-Joy said. "And the search *should* be hard."

"If it wasn't," one of her attendant females said, "she'd have every ragtag and bobtail wasting her time."

"You need to show commitment," another said. "That's why you should have brought a present."

"He's brought his painful paws," Young-Joy said. "I think that's commitment enough for tonight. Besides, I don't get to see many sturdy young bloods these days."

"But young males are all crude," an attendant snarled.

"No need to be so dogmatic," Young-Joy said, showing her yellow teeth. "And I need a little light relief sometimes. Wisdom, wisdom, wisdom—that's all you females ever want. Back off."

The attendants backed off but they grumbled and groused among themselves. Young-Joy, however, stretched herself out and sighed. Supporting her heavy head on her forepaws she studied me with her gleaming gold eyes. "Come on then, Rover, spit it out."

So I told her about my hungry night and my dream. I told her about the rabbit with puppy eyes, my mother, the poisonous toad, and the pain in my tail.

"Interesting," she said. Then she closed her eyes.

She was silent for so long I was afraid she'd gone to sleep. I said, "It isn't so much the dream itself . . ."

"No?" She raised one eyelid. She seemed to be winking at me. "So you didn't seek me out to hear about the archetypal significance of toads?"

"Uh, no."

"Or to be told that puppy eyes indicate insecurity? Or about compensatory behavior? Or about the primal yelp of pain?"

"No."

"Good." She settled herself again. "If I hear another primal yelp today I'll scream."

"It's this feeling that my mother doesn't like me anymore," I said.

"Tell me about your mother. Was she the down-to-earth type?"

"I'd say so. She died when I was very young but she always stressed common sense and self-reliance."

"Mmmm," Young-Joy said. "I'd say your problem, Rover, is . . . a little temporary indigestion."

"That's all?"

"Don't be insulted."

"I'm not. I'm relieved."

"I didn't know your mother," Young-Joy said. "But I'll bet she would have told you never to go to bed with nothing but half a cheese sandwich in your stomach. That's just asking for trou-

ble. And I can tell you what your mother would probably have advised. She'd have said to go to a park and chew a little grass."

"Grass?"

"And a few clover leaves. It's unfashionable now, but it'll sort you out in no time."

The mention of clover leaves reminded me of a field my mother took me and my brothers to in the mornings when it was fresh with dew. I hadn't thought of it for years. And I realized what Young-Joy said was true. Chewing grass and clover was just the sort of thing my mother would have told me to do.

"I can tell you something else your mother would have said to you, Rover."

"What?"

"Self-reliance is important. But that doesn't mean you should be shy about asking for help. Life is a balance."

"I'll try to remember that."

She shifted her position. "Time for you to go."

"Before I go, is there anything I can do for you?"

"Good," she said, lifting her head. "Good to ask. Your mother would have approved." She squirmed. "As a matter of fact there is something."

"Name it."

"There's a flea halfway down my tail and I'm too stiff to twist around to reach it."

I set to work combing the hair on her tail with my teeth.

"Mmmmm," she mumbled sleepily. "And next time, Rover, don't be so distempered when you dream about chasing your tail. Think what it's going to be like when you can't anymore. That'll be the time to be distempered."

Getting On

THE NIGHT WAS heavy and hot and windless. There was a faint smell of rain to come, but it was like remembered love. It made the present worse because it reminded you how much better things could be.

Even the fleas were restless. They took turns crawling into my ears whenever I tried to sleep, so after a while I gave up on the z's. I went for a walk. I headed for the biggest river in town.

It wasn't really cooler there, but the sound of the fast-flowing water reinvigorated me. It's a funny old life when you need extra energy to be able to sleep. But I gave my ears a good scratch and started looking again for somewhere safe to curl up.

I was dogging it slowly along a wire fence when I heard high-pitched scraping sounds. And then I heard humans who were trying to talk without making much noise.

I turned the corner and took a look. I found a ragged hole in the fence and, inside, two human males dragging a stack of cardboard boxes. I couldn't understand their words, but they were fussing with each other. A van was parked on the street near the hole, and it was obvious that the humans and their boxes were headed for it.

I shouted at them, "What do you pitiful excuses for living creatures think you're doing? Anybody with half a brain could tell you're up to no good. Can't you find a way to keep alive without stealing from your fellow beings? Have you no scruples?"

I really threw myself into it. It was none of my business, of course, but I was awake when I should have been asleep so why should these two males have it easy? I explained to them that co-operative society would collapse if everybody was to behave the way they were. I explained that they both ought to do the honorable thing and stop breathing.

The two males put the boxes down. But at first it was only to make a few feeble efforts to shoo me away. However I reiterated the moral weakness of their position and explained that they were crazy if they thought I'd obey the likes of them. Before long they did quit on the whole thing. They ran for their van and drove into the night.

"You've made the right decision," I shouted after them. "You'll respect yourselves more in the morning."

But then someone shouted at me, "What's the racket? What's going on?"

"I just chased off two drops of human scum," I said. "No big deal."

But as the dog got closer he kept shouting. "This is my territory. I'll make chow out of any dog stupid enough to invade it."

I wasn't afraid of him, but I left anyway. The airless night was the kind that bred irritation and bad moods. I had no doubt that I could convince the dog that I'd saved him embarrassment by purging his territory of the two thieves. But where there is a dog inside a wire fence, there is often a human being not far behind. And there is no counting on the understanding of a human being, especially in hot, heavy weather. Especially if that human being is a night watchman and might be armed.

I SLEPT UNDER some bushes on the riverbank. By morning it still hadn't rained. I stayed near the water all day, looking around. There were several small factories, many with fences like the one the night before. And there were also some houses and a few stores. But a lot of the buildings were freshly boarded up, so perhaps it was an area that was earmarked for change.

In the middle of the day the rain came at last. It transformed life for the better. I felt so mellowed that I even let a human child befriend me. I played chase-sticks with it until the child got tired.

It went into a house and I was about to wander off, but then the child came back out with a plate of food and offered me one of its sandwiches. I like peanut butter, but the child was a skinny creature—you could see its ribs—so I pretended I was too full for a whole sandwich and made do with a few small pieces.

When the child was finished it took its plate back to the house. But then it came out again with a rope.

The whole human species seems to believe that everything can be owned, and I guess they get like that young. Maybe human beings can only cope with the world if they think they can tie it up. They certainly find it too hard to accept the independence of an independent dog who wants to stay that way. I made a swift departure.

I found some food in an alley and ate. And later I also found a female. She seemed friendly, but she was locked in a small pen. She said her owner always chose a mate for her rather than let her choose for herself.

She *said* she wanted to have a love litter for a change. But when claw came to scratch she couldn't be bothered to dig from her side when I began to dig from mine, so I left.

I could never be content to let some other creature decide who I mated with. But maybe the truth of the matter was just that she didn't feel that special buzz for me.

And so I passed an easy day. But when it grew dark again, I didn't settle down to sleep. I went back to the fence where I'd interrupted the two morally challenged human males.

I FOUND THE hole, patched roughly with chicken wire. I stood and listened until I was convinced that no one was moving around inside the fence. Then I called, softly, "Hey, dog." When I got no response I called louder, "Hey, dog!" But I really had to yell before I got an answer. I shouldn't have been surprised, considering the night before.

"What do you want?" the dog inside finally said.

"To talk to you," I said. "Now."

The dog came out. He was a big one, and he wasn't in a friendly frame of mind. "This better be important," he growled.

"Do you value your own skin?"

"What's that supposed to mean?"

"Last night," I said.

"What about it?" There was a pause. "Oh. Was that you?"

"Yeah."

"Well, what do you want from me? A tail wag?"

"You were asleep last night."

"Was I?"

"And you were asleep just now too, weren't you?"

"So what?" he snarled.

"I came back," I said, "because I thought I was going to find some young puppy who didn't know any better. I was going to do a good deed and tell him what human beings do to watchdogs who sleep on the job and don't wake up when someone breaks in. Even if the human being with them has gone to sleep on the job himself. But there's going to be no good deed with you, is there? You're too old and cranky to learn your lesson."

He didn't answer me at first. Then he said, "I can learn whatever anybody cares to teach me, except how to be young again. I go to sleep. I don't hear so well. I can't help it."

And suddenly I felt that I was as morally challenged as the

two young humans I'd scared away. "I'm sorry," I said. "I shot my muzzle off when I didn't know what I was talking about."

The old dog shook himself and sat down.

We both knew what would inevitably happen. On another night more young humans would break in and the dog wouldn't hear them. The watchman wouldn't hear them either, but when he discovered the theft in the morning, he would blame the dog. He would say to his boss, "I tried to fight them but they were too strong for me. And the damn dog slept through the whole thing."

Instead of getting a new human, the boss would get a new dog. And get rid of the old one.

I poked at the fence. "I can help you get out of here tonight."

"To do what? Scrounge at the dump?"

Not everyone is cut out to be independent, but there's plenty of food around once you know where to look. "Not necessarily," I said.

"I can get myself out, when the time comes," he said.

I nodded. "Okay."

"I was a police dog, you know."

"Yeah?"

"From a puppy, trained for it, and I was good too. They treat you well as a police dog. When you're good at it. They do everything for you."

It seemed that he was saying he didn't think he'd survive long outside. And maybe he was right.

"Thanks for last night," he said. "The humans here think I frightened the thieves off. They made a big fuss of me."

"Glad to help," I said.

"And we don't get many break-ins."

"It's a credit to your reputation," I said. "Well, I'm on my way. Be lucky."

"Thanks." He got up and walked back to where he slept.

Maybe he was making the right decision. Maybe the area would be redeveloped and he would be retired to a comfortable doghouse and regular meals.

I just hope when my time comes, I'll manage to find a way to do it with some dignity.

Bridging

THE AIR HAD the freshness that comes after overdue rain. Although it was late, the moon was bright and I wasn't feeling sleepy, so I decided to cross the big river and go to a park I know that is full of flowers. I love flowers after a rain.

I saw him as I trotted onto the bridge. I stopped in my tracks. Not because there was another dog but because this dog was standing on the parapet looking over the edge. He was still, leaning forward the way a pointer does. Or the way a dog does if he is smelling a flower. But there was no flower. Only the darkness below, and the furious sound of the rain-swollen river.

I didn't want to startle him in case he toppled over the edge. I approached slowly and cleared my throat before I said, "Hi."

He said nothing.

"Something interesting down there? Mind if I take a look?"

"Leave me alone," he said. "Cross the damn bridge. Do whatever you do on the other side."

"Come on. Lighten up. Things can't be that bad."

He turned to face me. The streetlights reflected in his eyes like points of fire. He snarled, "What do you know about it?"

"I live in the same world you do, friend."

"You think so?"

"Sure. What's the problem? Are you hungry?"

"No, I'm not hungry."

"You can't be thirsty after all this rain, so it must be love."

"Have you got some compulsion to interfere in things that are none of your business? Is that *your* problem?"

"There is something in what you say."

"So go help somebody else."

"The river isn't going anywhere," I said. "It'll still be there when you want it. Why don't you tell me what's eating you."

"I just can't stand it here anymore, all right? Every place I go is crowded with human beings. You can't get away from them and their damn noise."

As if to prove his point, a car with a howling siren drove past us on the bridge.

"So?" I said. "It was that way yesterday too."

"And it'll be that way tomorrow," he said intently. "Or worse."

"You're right," I said. "It gets worse and worse."

"You'd think they were deaf, all the noise they make."

"Guess you better jump."

He frowned at me for a moment. Then he pointed again to the darkness beneath the bridge.

"But make sure you hit the water headfirst."

He turned away from the void again. "What are you talking about?"

"The last dog I knew who jumped off this bridge hit the water sideways. He broke one of his legs and cracked some ribs. He hurt too much to do anything but let the water carry him, and he washed up on the shore."

"And?"

"He was resting there when a couple of cats found him. He didn't have the strength to fight them."

"You mean they killed him?"

"Not right away," I said. "You know how cats are, how death is a game with them."

I thought I saw a shudder pass down his back.

"These two cats had just taken their first bites when I showed up. I chased them off, of course, and in his last breaths the dog told me what had happened."

"He was alive, and they were eating him?"

"Tie my tail and hope to die," I said. "Oops."

He said nothing, but he looked over the edge of the bridge, then back to me.

"But you've probably done a lot of diving," I said. "You probably know exactly the right angle to hit the water at."

A big red truck with another howling siren approached us and passed. The dog on the parapet watched it disappear into the night. His ears quivered.

"What a terrible sound," I said. "They're forever chasing each other around, human beings, each one making more of a racket than the last."

"Yeah," the dog said.

"Sometimes I think about what the world would be like if we were in charge."

"We?"

"Dogs," I said. "What do you think? We could make it better, couldn't we?"

"We'd have to get rid of *them* first," he said.

"All of them, do you think? Or would you keep a few as pets, as long as they were under control at all times, on leashes."

"All of them."

"Okay, all of them," I said. "And what would be the best way to get rid of them?"

"Eat them."

"They'd sure keep us in meat for a while. But are they any good? Have you ever tasted one?"

"No."

"Me neither. I've bitten a few but never gone, you know, the whole human. It never seemed quite the thing to do."

"They're not clean," he said.

"No?"

"You ever seen one lick itself?"

"I never have."

He didn't seem to have anything more he wanted to say on that subject, so I said, "If it turns out that they don't taste good then we'll have to do things like spay all the females."

"And neuter all the males," he said with a harsh laugh. "I could put my heart into neutering some of the males I've known."

"Given you a bad time, have they?"

"Yeah. You could say that."

"Still, you look in pretty good shape now."

"Yeah."

"And you *are* free."

He was silent.

"I mean, maybe you have an owner somewhere, but you're not on a leash tonight, are you? You may have a doghouse, but you don't have to go back to it."

"No," he said, "tonight I'm free."

"Tell you what," I said. "I was heading for a park just the other side of the bridge. It's big, and quiet, and there are nice flowers there this time of year. Are you into flowers?"

He didn't answer me.

"Why don't you come along?"

He stood silently on the parapet.

"My name's Rover. What's yours?"

He gave a little snort. "They called me Rover too."

"Well, Rover Two, you want to come into the park with me? The bridge will still be here. The river isn't going anyplace."

He hesitated. Then he crouched to jump down to the sidewalk. But at that moment an ambulance sped onto the bridge. It shrieked fiercely. It passed right by us.

Rover Two said, "Why do they sound one note when they're coming toward us and then sadder when they're past and going away?"

I shrugged. "They just do. It's the way things are."

"Yeah." Rover Two stood up. He turned away from me and he jumped off the bridge.

I could hardly believe it. My legs gave way beneath me and I dropped to the sidewalk. I felt a part of me had gone over the edge with him. And there was too much noise around to tell when he hit the water.

What had he said that I could argue with? Nothing. So why

didn't I want to go over the edge too? If another of the screaming monsters had gone past would I have jumped too?

No.

There may be precious little chance that things in the world will get better, but there's no chance at all if you're not here. You can't win if you're not in the game.

When I felt steadier I got up. Then I headed away from town, to where the air was still fresh and carried the scent of flowers.

The Elk

I WAS OUT past the big river. I'd spent the day sweet-talking two females but when sniff came to shove neither of them was interested. Nothing gained, but nothing really lost. I like getting acquainted, talking, flirting. You never know. Maybe on another day . . .

By the time they went home, I had decided not to cross the bridge back to town before I slept. Instead I spent the evening nosing around territory I'd never examined before, and that's how I came to be on a large parking lot that was new to me. Not that parking lots have much to offer, but on the far side of this one there was a long, white wall, and walls are always worth a look.

Halfway across the lot I heard an uncanine howl behind me. I stopped and turned and watched as an ambulance roared by.

It's curious how human beings—who consider themselves so superior—choose to imitate dogs when the going gets tough.

But as the ambulance passed into the night I heard another howl. This one was not artificial but neither was it a dog, at least not a dog with any accent I had ever heard. As I stood and listened, the new voice was picked up by a second and then a third and a fourth, all animals with the same strange inflections. And the mysterious music came from behind the wall. It was an exciting discovery. It needed examination.

However the wall was too high to jump, and the asphalt surface at its foot meant I couldn't dig beneath it. But my experience is that much of what human beings make is for show. Often as not, what looks impenetrable from the front has gaps at the back.

So I followed the wall at a trot and, sure enough, eventually I got to a place where brick gave way to wire. The fence was still high, but at the base there was earth. I dug a hole and soon I was on the other side.

Within a few strides I began to scent creatures I had never smelled before. Lots of them. Putting two and two together I realized I was in a zoo. Of course I'd heard of zoos but I'd never been inside one.

I shouted out, "Who was that who was singing to the ambulance siren?" When there was no answer, I shouted again, "The harmonies sounded good. I'd like to meet you."

And then I heard a deep voice, not far away. It said, "Looks like an admirer you got, Crista."

I followed the voice.

I passed amazing scents. I heard strange sounds. There was hardly any light, but the real creatures could not have been more exotic than those I imagined.

I called, "Hello? Hello?"

And that's how I met the wolves.

They were behind a high iron fence. The deep-voiced wolf said, "Well, well, well. Who be this?"

"I've come in from outside," I said. "They call me Rover."

The second wolf, a female, said, "It do sound like we got us a city cousin, Ayolf."

"You be right, I think, Crista," Ayolf said.

I said, "I was outside the zoo and I heard you howl. Were you just singing along, or are you in trouble? If it's trouble maybe there's something I can do for you."

"He think he can help our troubles, Ayolf," Crista said.

"I be all right, Crista," Ayolf said. "Be you all right?"

"I be all right, Ayolf."

"So who got troubles then? You got troubles, Call Me Rover?"

"No," I said.

"So nobody got no troubles," Crista said. "What a fine world this be."

"I'll sing to that," Ayolf said. "Do city cousin sing without he got troubles?"

"I like to sing," I said.

So we did, and Crista joined us. And so did other wolves nearby. We made quite a choir.

When we finished I said, "So you're happy here?"

"Happy?" Ayolf said. "He ask if we be happy, Crista. Be you happy?"

"Happyish," Crista said. "And you, Ayolf?"

"You know," Ayolf said, "I yearn. That's what I do. I yearn. If I yearn, can I be happy? What do you say, Call Me Rover? Be I happy if I yearn?"

"It depends what you yearn for," I said.

"Ah, it do depend," Ayolf said. "It do depend."

"What do you yearn for, Ayolf?" I asked.

"I yearn, I yearn for the chase and snap of life on the tundra. I yearn to track reindeer."

"Reindeer, Ayolf?" Crista said.

"And, yes, remember you that elk I brought down?"

"You never tire of telling about the elk," Crista said. "But it weren't you who brought it down."

"It weren't, Crista?"

"It were your grandfather, Ayolf. You be born here. You been here all your life."

"So I been, so I been. But still I yearn for the elk, the elk."

"It must be in the genes, Call Me Rover," Crista said. "He have it strong."

"My father told about that elk," Ayolf said. "I remember now. You be right as always, Crista. I remember my father tell how he ate from that elk. His father's pack tracked it, his father brought it down. My father were a cub, and he ate of the elk, and I be of him. So I yearn."

"But here be the rub, Call Me Rover," Crista said. "Ayolf wouldn't know how to track an elk."

"How hard can it be?" Ayolf asked. "Maybe Call Me Rover know. Have you ever tracked an elk, Call Me Rover?"

"No," I said. "I've never tracked an elk."

"There be an elk not a hundred bounds from where we stand," Ayolf said sadly. "That way."

I looked, but it was too dark to see anything. And there were so many confusing scents, so many new to me, that I had no idea which was elk.

"That be your idea of tracking?" Crista chided. "Point your nose? Some wolf."

"Don't make small of me, female," Ayolf said. "I be not on the tundra with an elk throat in my clamplike bite, but at least I be saving the specie."

"Ah, the specie," Crista said.

"That's what we do all day here, Call Me Rover," Ayolf said. "Save specie."

"Oh," I said.

"It be not so bad here," Crista said.

"No, not so bad. We feed. We breed. It be not so bad. We owe it to the specie to stay, I suppose." Ayolf sounded wistful, though.

"To tell the truth, Call Me Rover," Crista said, "if you open the elk run and drive an elk our way, big brave Ayolf here would run a mile."

"Nonsense," Ayolf said.

"Not nonsense," Crista said.

"Nonsense. You know full well," Ayolf said. "Because we have no mile to run."

"You sound tired," Crista said. "Be you tired?"

"I be tired. Saving the specie all day. It make a wolf tired."

"It been nice to meet you, Call Me Rover," Crista said. "Stop again sometime."

"Tell him to drive the elk here," Ayolf said. He was already on his way to their lair.

"Yes," Crista said, "next time, you drive an elk here, Call Me Rover."

"All right," I said. "I'll try."

Crista leaned through the fence and lowered her voice. "Just make sure it be a small one, eh?"

Princess

RAIN BROUGHT NEW air that was fresh and cool, and I found myself in the mood to try a feeding place I don't often use. It's in a shopping center well away from the middle of town.

The center's discarded food is left in a basement at the bottom of a ramp. Most of the time a metal barrier blocks the way in. And when the weather is hot, the air in the basement is foul. Yet if you're inclined to risk a place where there is only one way in and out, the rewards can be great. Once I found a whole sheep's leg there without a single other dog around. Full belly, no hassle, good bone. The stuff of dreams.

So, invigorated by the cooler weather, I found the shopping center. I have a strategy. What I do is wait near the top of the ramp until I see one of the trucks that collect the trash. When the humans inside raise the barrier for truck to back in, I nip underneath it. Then—and this is where I've thought the situation out in a way that a lot of other dogs wouldn't—then I hide in the basement until the truck has left again.

When a truck leaves, the humans who supervise the basement leave too, and they don't return until the next collection truck is about to arrive. Human beings love cycles and timetables. Moreover, the truck that's just left has taken out what's been waiting longest. That leaves a patient dog alone with the fresher discarded material. I eat my fill, hide again when I hear the basement humans returning, and leave underneath the next truck.

I waited at the shopping center until a truck pulled in. I tucked myself under it. Once in the basement I hid. I watched as the truck was loaded and began to pull out. The last human in the basement stood at a control panel with his hand on a button, ready to lower the metal barrier.

And then, to my utter astonishment, a dog from outside trotted down the ramp, right past the collection truck. Talk about reckless.

I suppose I should have left the idiot dog to his fate, but a dog is a dog, however stupid, however irresponsible. I jumped out of my hiding place and ran for the ramp. I shouted, "If you value your life, get out now!"

I'll say this for him, he didn't dither. He turned as I shot past him, and when I finally stopped running in a schoolyard near the shopping center, the idiot dog was by my side. I sat to catch my breath in the shade of some bushes. He sat too. He was a young dog but no pup.

He said, "I take it you've saved me from a danger to life and paw. I'm grateful for your generosity, but I am totally mystified as to what took place. Please explain it to me."

I said, "They don't like 'strays' back there."

"No?"

"If a human being sees you, he pushes a button and a metal fence rolls down over the entrance."

The idiot dog wasn't completely stupid. "And so you're trapped?"

"And they call the dogcatchers."

"But that's awful," he said. "It's like we're . . . vermin or something."

"Human beings can't bear what's out of their control. They think that the only good dog is a dog they feed themselves. Any other dog is dangerous."

"I hadn't thought of it that way," the idiot dog said.

"You better reproduce yourself quickly, chum," I said. "Because on today's form you're not going to have the time to get many chances."

"Perhaps not, perhaps not." He leaned back. He looked into the sky. "Don't you love watching the clouds?"

As it happens, I do, but I didn't say anything. I didn't want to encourage him.

Then the idiot dog said, "Have you reproduced yourself?"

"What?"

"Do you have pups?"

"Some."

"Do you know them?"

"Have you just landed? Because you don't talk like someone who has been independent in this world very long."

"But wouldn't you like to raise your own pups?" he said. "Wouldn't you like to know them as they grow up? Help them when they meet their first human being? Teach them how to cope?"

"Life isn't like that," I said. But I began to realize that this was an unusual young dog, however idiotic. He had dreams.

He said, "I want to know my own pups. I yearn for it. My quest is to find a like-minded female. A female who has the same vision I do. A female who wants to share a family life. Who wants to become a pack of two with me."

"Sounds like you've got a touch of the human disease," I said. "Control. Because it sounds like you want a female who will do things the way you say."

"No no," he protested. "I'm ready, eager, to look after the litter, when it comes, while my beloved takes time for herself, has some space of her own. But I seek the knowledge, the strength, of being certain that she'll be back. Of being sure that when the weather turns cold, she'll warm me and I'll warm her. That's what I'm looking for. Someone who will value my attention. Someone I can be a prince to, someone who will be a princess to me."

"Well, good luck," I said. "I hope you don't have too many cold nights before you find her."

"Thank you for your kind wishes," he said. Then, "There she is! There she is!"

"Where?"

"Up there. All I need is a way to get her down from the sky."

I looked up. But I couldn't distinguish the cloud he was pointing at from all the others.

Meanwhile he cried, "Come down to me, my princess. Join me. I am here. I am waiting for you. Come to me. Come to me."

Maybe I was a romantic once. Because whenever I hear the poetry of the impractical, something deep inside me responds. But my life now is focused on how the world really is. For instance, working out that it's not a great idea to spend too much time with a dog who is baying at a cloud when one is still near a shopping center where there are frustrated dogcatchers.

And then somebody shouted, "Halloo!"

I turned to look, but my romantic idiot dog friend kept crying to the sky, "Join me, my princess!"

"It's been a long time since I was called a princess," the voice behind us said, and a female emerged from the other side of the bushes. As it happened I already knew her.

The romantic youngster was smitten. "I have asked," he cried, "and she has come down from the sky and answered. What a glorious day!"

"Hey, my name is Gloria," she said. "What's yours, handsome?" Then she nodded to me. "Hello, Rover."

"Gloria," I said.

"I heard your little friend calling. I like the sound of him."

"He's a nice guy," I said.

She turned to the romantic. "If you're a nice guy who wants to be nice to me, I'll be waiting over by the walnut tree." She left us.

"I think I'm in love," the romantic said.

"Look, chum," I said. "I'm not one to bad-muzzle anybody, but I've got to say, Gloria is not everyone's idea of a princess. I saw her bite clean through the leg of a little dog in an alley garbage pile. She didn't even give him a warning growl. Nobody—nobody—would have taken that little dog's intrusion as a challenge rather than stupidity. Certainly no litter-sharing princess."

"Rover," the romantic said, "you saved my life today. And I know you mean well. But just as fate provided you, fate has provided Gloria. Maybe she has a mean streak, but my love can change all that."

"If you say so," I said. "I don't claim to be an expert on princesses."

"Nor I, yet," he said. "But maybe one day I will be. And if not it certainly won't be for lack of trying. You've got to be prepared to kiss a lot of frogs if you want to find a princess."

He trotted off to join Gloria, not quite as much an idiot dog as I had taken him for.

Love

HE WAS IN an old house, and if it hadn't been late at night and quiet, I probably would have trotted by without noticing. As it was, I only just made out his sobs.

I stopped by the roadside to listen, still not sure if I had heard anything at all. But I had, and within a few moments I found him. I couldn't see him at first, but I could smell the blood.

"Hey, what's the problem?" I said.

He didn't answer, but he stopped sobbing.

"I asked a question. What's going on?"

"Please, don't hurt me," he whined.

"Don't be pathetic," I said. "Are you a human or a dog?"

"A dog," he said, though if I didn't have acute hearing I might not have made out the words.

"And are you in trouble or not?"

"I'm in trouble," he said.

IT TOOK SOME coaxing to get him out into the moonlight where I could get a good look at him. He was young, barely out of puppyhood. And he had bites and cuts all over his body. But worse was he didn't care. He had given up.

"What happened to you?" I said.

"There were four of them," he said. "I wasn't doing anything bad. Just looking for something to eat. I found a plastic bag in the street and I was scratching at it. The next thing I knew they were all around me and calling me names and nipping me and I couldn't tell which way to turn or what I should do. When I tried to run they caught me and pulled me down and bit me and kept on and on and on and there was nothing I could do but curl up tight and finally they went away."

"The kind of pack that gives independent dogs a bad name," I said. I do loathe dogs who make other dogs their sport.

"It was awful," the pup said. He started to whimper again.

"When was the last time you ate?"

"A couple of days ago."

"All right," I said. "You go inside. I'll find you something to eat. But while I'm away, start licking yourself into shape. You're a mess."

BEHIND A FRIED chicken store I gathered enough castoffs to make a meal. By the time I got back, my young acquaintance was already brighter. He would have torn into the scraps if I hadn't insisted that he slow down and be careful. Chicken bones can splinter in the throat.

When he was done he said, "Thanks."

I said, "You have a collar. Why aren't you tucked up in a warm doghouse somewhere?"

"I followed a female," he said.

And suddenly a lot of things became clearer. I laughed.

"It's not funny. I was crazy about her."

"I'm sure you were."

"But at first she wouldn't let me get close," he said. "And when she finally did, we were so far away from home that I didn't know how to get back."

"And how long ago was all this?"

"Four days. Maybe five."

"And look at the state of you." I laughed again.

"Haven't you ever been in love?" he snapped.

"You've got to know how to handle it, pup."

"I'm not a pup!"

"You are to me," I said.

HE WAS YOUNG. He was strong. He recovered quickly. The vicious pack hadn't done real damage to anything but his self-esteem, and even that can heal.

I let him travel with me for a couple of days. I showed him some of the places that can be relied on for food. I taught him to check who else was around before he started to fill his snout.

We even picked up the scent of the pack that had roughed him up. He wanted us to teach them a lesson.

"Fight four dogs?" I said.

"I bet you could take them all by yourself," he said, "but I'd help." He was feeling better. It was time to cut him loose.

Then, later the same afternoon, I could tell he was in a funny mood. We were resting as the sun neared the horizon, and instead of chattering, he was quiet.

"Are you all right?" I said.

He didn't speak at first. Then he said, "Yeah."

"Remembering life at your owner's house?"

He snorted. "You think you know everything, don't you?"

"No. But I know that some dogs are cut out for the independent life, and some aren't."

He thought about that for a while. He said, "Do you know what I miss most?"

"The two square meals a day?"

"Besides the food."

"What?"

"I've got this great blanket in my basket."

"Yeah?"

"And I miss the television."

"Well," I said, "I think it's about time you went home, don't you?"

He looked at me.

"Don't you want to go home?" I said.

"More than anything in the world."

THIS PUP WAS so green that he thought I was saying I could take him to his house. Now how was I supposed to do that? Even if he described the house, like the human beings inside, they all look pretty much the same to me.

"But I don't know where my house is," the pup whined. "If I'd known how to get there I'd have gone days ago."

"You don't have to know how to get there," I said. "Not if you're smart. Not if you're willing to take a bit of a chance."

He stared at me. "Anything."

"Come on," I said.

WE WENT TO a neighborhood where there were a lot of houses.

"I don't get it," he said. "So there are houses. So what?"

"You have a collar, right?"

"Yeah."

"And it has a metal plate on it."

"It does?"

"So your collar will tell somebody where your home is. All we have to do is find the right somebody to take a look."

"But how do we do that?"

"We find a child," I said. "Then you follow it home, and you sit outside being as cute and friendly as you know how. You wag your tail off. The child will bully its parents wanting to keep you. In order to get rid of you, the parents will read your collar and take you back to where you came from."

"Wow," the pup said. Then, "Will it work?"

I said, "It's possible that the child will win and the parents will give you a new home. If that's what happens, decide if you like it. If you don't, run away and find another child."

"You make it sound so simple," the pup said.

"Life is simple," I said, "if you do it right."

AFTER A WHILE we found a child on its own. It seemed about the right age, and it was clean, which suggested it had parents and wasn't independent. "There you go, pup. Chocks away."

"Thank you for the help, Rover. I'll never forget you."

"That'll feed me on a regular basis all right."

"I know I sound silly to you," he said. "But are you so cynical about everything?"

"Sure," I said.

The truth is far more complicated than that, but there is no way to explain the subtleties of life to a pup who has lost his way home for love.

Space

I WAS IN a big park on the south side of town when I noticed a dog who seemed to be afraid of every sound and movement near him. He jumped back from things as innocent as a blue jay landing on the branch of a tree, a Frisbee dropping on the ground yards away, and a human child giggling as it walked with its mother.

The dog appeared whole, with no limp, and his coat was shiny. He was a good size—not as big as me, but muscular—and neither young nor old. He looked to be in the prime of life. Why should a creature like that—a creature like me—be so skittish?

I went over to ask. "Hey," I said.

He twisted to face me and bared his teeth.

"Oh, for Dog's sake, put 'em away," I said. "I'm just being so-
ciable. I've been watching you and——"

"Why have you been watching me?" he snarled.

"Because I thought you might be in trouble," I said.

"What trouble?" he snapped.

"But up close I realize the real problem is that you were abandoned as a puppy and raised by cats and it's left you with an in-
curable personality disorder. No way I can help you with that.
Have a good life." I turned on my pads and headed away.

IT WAS A dark day, but although the sky was cloudy, there were
pillows of white among the gray. So if you wanted to, you could
say it promised better.

I wanted to. I wanted to feel the sun warming the fur on my
back. I wanted to feel a tickling breeze on my belly. So I expected
it to happen that way. Why not?

Life seems divided between those of us able to look for the
bright side and those who always look for the dark. It's not that
I don't understand the dark siders. There are certainly more
dogs suffering for no good reason nowadays than ever before. It's
because there are more human beings around than ever before.

I don't object to human beings in principle any more than I
object to, say, squirrels. As long as a human being minds its own
business and leaves me to mind mine, I have no complaint.

But it doesn't seem natural for human beings to let things be.
They're forever hurrying, or destroying, or replacing. They act
like they're cornered all the time. They fight whatever gets in
their way. I know they're supposed to be intelligent, but the evidence for that seems incomplete to me. They're very good with
their paws but so are squirrels. I'd like to see a human being that

can do half the things a squirrel can. And however intelligent human beings are, they're not smart enough to know when to leave things alone.

I found some trees by a stream in the park. I sat and watched a couple of squirrels for a while. The sun came out. It felt good on my back.

"Hey."

I looked around and found the fearful dog. I said, "If you want hassle, go bother someone else."

"No, no," he said. "I want to apologize, for being off with you before."

" 'Off with me'?" I said. "Where are you from?"

"Not around here," he said with feeling.

I saw that he had a collar and that a metal tag hung from it and swung free. In this town metal plates are stapled to the collars of dogs with owners. "Where are your humans?" I asked him.

"They gave me away."

"Why?"

"They had a baby. I admit, I didn't think it was a good idea, because it was so shrieky. But I would have gotten used to it. I'm sure I would. Only they didn't give me a chance. Instead they brought me to . . . this place."

"And abandoned you?"

"No," he said. "I have new owners. They're the parents of my old ones and they have my basket, my ball, my leash, my everything. I belong to them now. But I can't bear it."

I yawned and stretched. I shook myself in the fresh breeze. "You don't look like you've been starved or beaten. What's so bad about the new owners?"

"It's not them, the humans. It's this place," he said. "It's not . . . home."

"Where is home?"

"That way." He nodded to the east.

"And what's so different about it?"

"Oh, everything," he said. "It's taller . . ."

"You mean bigger, more space?"

"No," he said, snapping the word the way he had when I first saw him. "Taller." He looked into the sky. "And lots more humans."

That surprised me. This town already has more humans than I could count. It was hard to imagine what a denser aggregation of them would be like. Except that it would be no place for a rational dog.

"It is so quiet here," he said. "I'm going crazy."

A squirrel ran up a tree behind him. He whirled and growled at it. Then he sat down sadly. "And there's so much emptiness here. How can anyone possibly guard it?"

"Wait, wait," I said. "I don't understand. You come from a noisy place that you guard, and that has a lot more human beings, but much less space to run around in?" It sounded like hell to me.

"Where I come from everything is up and down," he said.

I looked at the squirrel, perched on a branch in the tree. I looked back at the fearful dog.

He said, "The humans there live in stacks going up into the sky. And it's all . . . under control. We only got weather when we took them out for a walk. But my owners here leave me outdoors for hours on end. I get wet. I get hot. What is it going to be like when the weather turns cold?"

"So you ran away from your new owners?"

"Yes," the fearful dog said.

"How long ago?"

He paused to think. "Two days."

"I bet you're hungry."

"I certainly am. Do you know where they keep the bowls around here?"

Oh my wagging tail! "Yeah. We have big bowls, but we call them bins."

I took him to the back of a steak restaurant. It wasn't the closest place that humans dump the food they don't want, but in the neighborhood it was the least likely to offend the fastidious.

I tipped over a bin for my new acquaintance. When he didn't seem to know what to do next, I ripped the plastic bag and found him a choice bone.

He sniffed it carefully. "But this is meat," he said.

"Sure."

"I don't eat meat."

"What?"

"Ever since I was weaned they've fed me vegetarian pellets. They're rough when they're dry but they soften up wonderfully in cream."

"No pellets here, friend. Sorry."

He sniffed the bone again.

I said, "Have you ever tried meat?"

"Well, no."

"Are you hungry?"

He nodded.

"Well?"

He looked at the bone, but he left it. He stuck his snout into the plastic bag. When he came out he had half a burger. He took a tiny bite and chewed. He stopped and thought about it. "This is closer," he said. He tried another nibble. "But it's still so . . . so . . . animal." He stood over the rest of the burger. He looked to the east. "I need to go home."

"Do you know your way?"

"I watched out the window as they drove," he said. "I'll know."

"Is it far?"

"Yes. Very far."

"And you're not going to eat any of this meat?"

He looked at the burger again. "I don't think I can."

"Then I think you'd better get on your way."

He nodded and left, walking east, a dog who didn't like bones—is there nothing that humans don't want to change?

There was no knowing, of course, whether he would make it home. But I looked on the bright side. I decided that he would make it and be welcomed and live to a ripe old age. After all, he was making an effort to solve his own problem. That was an attitude that deserved reward.

Human Management

IT WAS HOT and sunny, but with a refreshing breeze. I was in the largest park in town, ambling from picnic site to picnic site, when I heard some human beings shout. I looked up and saw a tiny female. She was strutting through the middle of an area where some humans were playing with sticks and balls.

The humans shouted at her, but they all stopped what they were doing until she was out of the way on the other side.

I met her there. "Hey," I said, "you ought to watch yourself."

The female stood, gave herself a glance, and said, "I don't think I'll bother. You watch me instead. Okay, big boy?"

She was the smallest dog I'd ever met, though she looked bigger than she was, with large batlike ears and more fur by volume than all her flesh. I said, "Are you looking for trouble? If those humans hadn't stopped their game you might easily have been seriously injured."

"But they did stop their game." She laughed, then she lay down in the grass and rolled on her back. When she was upright again she said, "Ah, that's better. If I get an itch it drives me *mad* if I can't get at it for a scratch. What did you say your name was?"

"Rover."

"And so very you, if you don't mind my saying so. Large, and strong, and roughly handsome. And you have a scent with considerable gravitas."

"Thank you," I said.

"My name is Jezebel. Yes, you're a fine dog, Rover. But independent, unless I miss my guess, aren't you, poor thing."

"What do you mean, 'poor thing'?" I said.

"Oh but *darling,* you miss out on so much if you're independent."

"I eat well. I go where I like. And," I added, "I get to meet the most interesting dogs . . ."

"But owning a human being is absolute heaven, darling, if you know how."

"I thought it was the humans who owned the dogs," I said.

"Your perceptions seem sadly askew," she said. "But perhaps you've had a few unfortunate experiences with human beings. Is that it?"

"It's safe to say that I've had unfortunate experiences with them."

"Darling, you should be more positive about humans. You'd have a lot more fun."

"Fun is not a word I associate with them."

"It's not that they're fun in themselves, but they can save you so much time. Think about it. How long do you spend each day scrounging up your food?"

"How long?"

"That was the question, darling, yes."

"Well, it depends how lucky I am and what I feel like eating. There's plenty of food around. I almost never go hungry."

"But you're proving my point entirely!"

"How?"

"You have to *think* about it, darling. Whereas if you owned the right sort of human the food would be there twice a day, automatically."

"And if I don't like what they give me?"

"You don't eat it, of course. And you complain until they give you what you want. Dear oh dear! You don't know the first thing, do you? Darling, in my household they feed me off their own plates. They take me *into* restaurants and have a plate laid for me at the table. Now that beats fighting other dogs for scraps out back, wouldn't you say?"

"I've never eaten at the table in a restaurant, that's true," I said.

"My human feeds me asparagus off his own plate. He holds it, dripping with butter, and all I have to do open my mouth and chew. Have you ever *tasted* asparagus, Rover dear? Dripping with butter. The soft green tips . . ." She licked her chops at the thought and her huge eyes became dreamy.

She was making me feel hungry. And I admit it, she was making me wonder if maybe she had a point. But I said, "I just don't see myself coming and going at the whim of a human being."

"Darling, who does?"

"Well, you do. Don't you?"

"Am I here, lying in the sun? Or am I locked in a pen somewhere?" She shook her thick golden mane impatiently. "I never go anywhere I don't want to go. It's a matter of letting them know who's boss and speaking up for yourself. Do you know how to speak up for yourself?"

"I can make myself heard," I said.

"Mmmm, yes, but probably you shout, and that alarms humans. I find them to be rather nervous creatures. You must never frighten them, if you want to get the best out of them. Never. Quiet discipline, and a touch of charm if you can muster it, that's the ticket."

"If you say so."

"I do, Rover, I do. Although I concede that I have a natural advantage, being small and pretty. But you have a rough charm too, you know."

"Oh yes?"

"Now you're fishing for compliments, darling. Let's just say that I'm certain that you've got sufficient of what it takes to get good service from the right human beings. And being looked after would free up so much time for you."

"To do what?"

"Anything. Everything. For instance, my dear, have you ever ridden on a bus?"

"A bus?"

"One of those large motored vehicles that——"

"I know what a bus is."

"I ride on them all the time."

"Why?"

"To see the world, of course!" She batted at a fly that was buzzing around her ear. "Buses have places they stop. If you wait there until one comes, you can get on it. As long as you act like you belong there the humans on the bus accept it. 'Look at the cute little dog,' they say. 'She's riding the bus like she knows where it's going.' I've never been thrown off. Not once."

"You can understand what humans say?"

"Not the actual words, but the meaning is clear. They're terribly transparent, poor darlings. Not that I rode a bus here today. My house borders this park. And I like to do a little walking now and again. When the weather's right."

"If you get on a bus and go somewhere," I said, "how do you get back home?"

"Wherever there's a bus stop to go somewhere, there's one to go home on the other side of the street. But if I get in trouble, I just go to the biggest house I can find. They look at my necklace and they call my humans and my humans come and pick me up."

I checked her neck. "That's a collar," I said.

Jezebel sighed. "So handsome, but . . . I won't say stupid, darling, because who knows. But so *ignorant*. Look at my necklace, Rover. Look at the little jewels. Feel how soft the leather is. If I didn't like it, darling, I wouldn't wear it. It is, therefore——"

"A necklace," I said. I scratched myself behind the ear.

"You know," she said, "your negative attitude about human beings could even cost you your life. Oh yes, it might, so don't look at me as if I'm soft in the head. I'll tell you a story that might help you understand. It concerns a sister of mine called Sou Shi Pang of Bangor——Susie to friends and family. And Susie's human actually brought her back from the dead."

"Was her human a vet?" I asked.

"He was an ordinary human being that Susie had adopted and trained. Are you going to listen, Rover, or are you going to ask cynical questions?"

"I'm listening."

"Well, then pay attention, darling. Susie was my older sister, born three litters before me. And Susie was, not to put too fine a point on it, a little excitable." Jezebel fluffed her ruff gently before continuing. "One of Susie's eccentricities was the doorbell. She had only to hear a doorbell and she'd jump up, shouting, and run to the door. Such a waste of energy, Rover. All one has to do is wait and a human will see to it. But poor Susie thought she had to do everything herself. Well, one evening, when she was snoozing on her pillow, the doorbell rang and she leaped up and ran to the door, shouting her little throat hoarse. And she felt a pain in her chest. And then, darling, poor little Susie blacked out. Nothing. Absolutely nada, Rover. The big nap. Her poor little heart had stopped. She was gone."

"Oh dear."

"But, but—and this is the point of the story, Rover—Susie's human was there, and he couldn't *bear* to see her lying on the carpet, not breathing. So he picked her up and put her on the hall table and he breathed air back into her lungs. He massaged her chest too, and sure enough, Susie's heart started beating again and she lived for another whole year."

I must have looked skeptical because she said, "It's a true story, darling, Susie told me herself. And what I'm saying, Rover, is that if *your* heart stopped beating and you keeled over, you could miss out on another whole year of life. Or even two, big, strong, and handsome as you are. It's something to think about."

"I promise to think about it," I said.

Jezebel stretched and then scratched herself gently behind each of her feathery ears. "Well, I'm getting hungry." She looked up at me. "Come to dinner, darling, take potluck. There's always plenty."

"I'm not sure your humans would like that," I said.

"Have you been listening, Rover?" She tossed the hair out of her eyes. "What they like or dislike is immaterial."

"Still," I said, "I get edgy when I'm with humans. I don't have your skills."

"I'm sure you could learn."

"Maybe another time. Meanwhile, I'll make sure not to answer any doorbells."

"Well, just don't leave it too late, darling," Jezebel said. "Because it would be a crying shame for a nice, big, strong, handsome dog like you to die prematurely."

She rose and curled her plumed tail across her back. She shook herself so that all her golden hair fluffed and glistened. Then she strutted off, chin up, back through the middle of the humans' ball game.